Out
January 2024.

1° DEGREE NORTH

ACTION THRILLER

STEVE BRIDGER

Balloonview

First edition published in 2014

© Copyright 2014 Steve Bridger

Disclaimer
This book is a work of fiction, except in the case of historical fact, any resemblance to actual persons, living or dead, is purely coincidental.

Paperback ISBN 978-1-907798-59-7

Mobipocket/Kindle 978-1-907798-60-3

ePub ISBN 978-1-907798-61-0

Published in the UK by Balloon View Ltd, www.balloonview.com

Printed and bound in Great Britain by
CPI Group (UK) Ltd, Croydon, CR0 4YY

DEDICATION

Francis David Thomas Cobley
Ronnie Chapman
Mike Leeves

Thanks for their wonderful support

The Wastell Sisters
Penny Kenton-Russ
Maria Morris
The real Tom Hollamby
Steve Preston
Lyndsay Marie
Graham Howe - CGS

Acknowledgements

Singapore Straits Times
Singapore Press Holdings
UK Ministry of Defence
The Ton Class (Minesweepers) Association
Cover design by Sarah Harris:
www.sarahharris.daportfolio.com

ONE

30th July 1960. Pulau Tioman Island, Mersing, Malaya. The day before the Malayan Emergency ended.

Do you remember your first love? Do you remember the insane cocktail of chemicals rushing through your bloodstream, making your head spin, and your whole body tingle and pulsate with emotions so powerful they took your breath away? Do you remember the first, and possibly last time, you surrendered your heart and soul without limit, without constraint, without question?

Lee and Jannah lay in each other's arms, eyes closed, feeling the warmth of the sun, hearing the gentle waves of the South China Sea touch and sink, bibbling and tickling into the soft white sand. They put time on hold, freezing each second, capturing the moment and locking it safe inside their minds. This day on tropical Tioman Island was one they'd never forget. The young lovers had spent the morning snorkelling above the coral. Yellow tailed barracuda, puffer, angel and butterfly fish kissed a welcome through wide mouths as if they were blowing perfectly rounded smoke rings.

Now, Jannah's head was propped on a pillow of folded towels, totally relaxed. She'd loosened the straps of her bikini top and turned down the waistband to work on her tan. Her Chinese-Malay parentage had produced a woman of staggering oriental beauty. Lee was smitten the first time he'd laid eyes on her. They'd been together for two years, two remarkable years; Lee was twenty and Jannah nineteen. He let her doze. Lee chose that moment to take a stroll among the swaying palms fringing the beach.

'He's gone. Let's do it now'. Rifleman Alan Jenkins took another hefty swig of Johnnie Walker Red Label and grinned a salacious grin. 'He won't be any trouble.'

'We should toss to see who goes first.' Private Barry Snell was starting to palpitate with excitement. A silver dollar was flipped and spun high in the air. 'Heads or tails?'

'Whoever gets there first wins!' Jenkins was already stripped to his shorts and sprinting, kicking up sprays of sand, before the coin hit the ground.

***

The two British soldiers, members of the infamous Ferret Force, had come ashore further down the beach. They'd been spying, hidden in the undergrowth and twisted mangrove reeds. This was to be their last day in Malaysia before an overnight trip to Singapore, repatriation by RAF Transport Command to Lyneham and onward to their base in Aldershot. This was to be a last delicious memory of Malaysia before peace stopped play.

Alan Jenkins' shadow fell upon her before he did. Whisky fumes, body odour like rancid milk and dripping sweat signalled his arrival and malevolent intent. The red mist of lust and passion blinded him. In death, he remembered how Jannah had slowly opened her eyes and kept her body rigid as if she'd been waiting patiently, expecting him. Her hand moved at light-speed, grabbing the dagger hidden under the pillow of towels.

A vertical spear of steel welcomed his beating heart. The bait worked. The trap sprung. As she knew it would.

Barry, fuelled by Johnnie Walker, couldn't understand it. He saw Alan reach the woman to tear off her bikini, then slump into stillness without a sound. In the time it took Barry's brain to do a double-take, he'd lost his head. Lee's machete, honed to a razor's edge, severed spinal cord, larynx and jugular in a deadly arc of malice.

Barry's head bounced on the sand in a pumping geyser of blood, his startled expression forever unsure of what happened. The bodies were dragged down to the sea. Sharks turned the placid turquoise sea blood red, stripping skin to bone, destroying all evidence, removing any trace of the attackers ever being there. Two dismembered bodies ripped to shreds and returned to nature.

**

Vengeance runs deep. The contest for Malaya had lasted for over a generation. Lee's father Chia Jaya, was trained by the British to fight the Japanese at the Special Training School 101 before the fall of Singapore in 1942. Chia joined the fight against the Japanese, conducting guerrilla operations along the west coast of Malaya, from Kuala Lumpur down to Malacca and Johor.

Turn and turnabout. Following the Japanese defeat, the British returned to Malaya and Singapore expecting to pick up where they left off. Many Chinese, Malay and Asians who'd fought the Japanese had a different agenda. They wanted their own country and took up arms against the British, joining the military arm of the MCP - the Malayan Communist Party.

Jannah was an MCP unit commander. Daughters, mothers, wives and lovers fought alongside their male counterparts, sharing combat duties. The women were lethal warriors. Lee was her second in command. Together they made a formidable team, complementing each other's talents. Jannah supplied the tactical brains and cunning. Lee was a silent assassin, his victims only knowing they were dead when they reached the afterlife. Lee had the look and build of a Martial Arts film star with lean sinewy strength. Lee's reactions were faster than the beating of a hummingbird's wings. He had a thin vertical scar on his cheek below his left eye about an inch long, which made him look as dangerous as he was.

'Time to clean up, let's leave this beach to its beauty and sweep away the filth.' Jannah towelled herself dry after washing Jenkins' blood into the sea. 'Bastard! This is going to stain.' Jannah spoke without emotion, as if she'd spilled ketchup rather than lifeblood on her bikini.

'At least we're two Lee Enfield rifles richer.' Lee placed the soldiers' rifles by their cold beers in the ice box.

The business done; the young lovers reverted to a day out at the beach.

***

As they waited for the boat to take them off the island, their thoughts rolled back two weeks.

Their unit was holding out in the jungle near Kota Bharu, close to the border with Thailand. Jannah and Lee had made their way, unarmed, to the nearest village to contact known sympathisers and get food supplies. This area had recently been given White Status; an area free of communist terrorists. The introduction of I.D. cards and the central cooking programme where all rice was confiscated, cooked and allocated to the villagers, made smuggling to the communist guerrillas almost impossible. They were nearly starving.

There had been a palpable change in the villagers' attitude towards strangers, everyone was suspect. Bodies of dead fighters were slumped against walls as evidence of progress being made against the communists. Jungle warfare had turned dramatically against them with the arrival of the 'Ferret Force'.

The Ferret Force was formed from Force 136 special ops and seasoned Chindit veterans fighting in the Burmese jungle. Their mission was not to defeat the MCP but to sow absolute terror.

Taking prisoners was not their style. Dayak head-hunters from Borneo were their secret weapon. Dayaks were superbly talented trackers, as one with the jungle. Their job was to locate the enemy bases. The Ferret Force would set ambushes and annihilate anyone - man, woman or child caught in the net.

Jannah and Lee had no way of knowing an ambush had been set for their unit. As they left a shop holding bags of bread and cheese, a woman lost her footing, falling and twisting her ankle. Had they not gone to her aid, had they not been delayed, they too would've been caught in the crossfire.

It was carnage. Their comrades lay rigid in death. No time to mourn, only to flee. Jannah and Lee took the swiftest route south by stealing a boat. Two weeks later they'd arrived safely at Mersing, exhausted but alive. Word reached them of a peace agreement; the end of hostilities, the Malayan Emergency was over. Word too, that members of the Ferret Force would be on Tioman Island, relaxing on their last day in Malaya.

For Jannah and Lee it was the last chance for revenge.

***

Billy Chang was concerned.

He'd arranged to meet Alan and Barry at a quayside bar by the landing jetty. He knew they would be in a celebratory mood, but would not want to miss the flight home. Something was definitely wrong.

Under pressure from the British, the Canadian government allowed their Chinese community to join British military units. Their skill as guerrilla fighters and fluency with the language was in massive demand particularly for special operations.

Billy was dressed in an old pair of battered grey trousers and a dirty white vest. He was chunky, thickset, powerful but extremely light on his feet. He had penetrating eyes that were constantly vigilant. A mop of ruffled black hair gave him an unkempt appearance that helped him blend seamlessly with the local plantation workers and fishermen.

If you had x-ray vision you would have seen a Webley & Scott revolver concealed in his baggy slacks. The irony of his situation was not lost on Billy. Here he was, thousands of miles away from his family, fighting for respect and recognition back home in Canada. The communists in Malaya were fighting for freedom - and he was fighting them; just the way of the world.

He sat in a prime corner position to guard against a surprise attack from behind. The floor of the bar was covered in sand and dirt. The tables were filthy, sticky with spilt drink. The overhead ceiling fan limped round in a creaking circle of uselessness. The fetid odour of bad fish hung in the air, refusing to be budged by the pathetically sweeping blades.

Billy had an uninterrupted view of the waterfront, of fishermen arriving from a day on the water, and others getting ready for a night's fishing. A spluttering cough of an ancient marine diesel and a black cloud of exhaust smoke caught Billy's eye and raised a question in his mind. Why was an empty launch casting off at this time of night?

Billy was on his feet and reached the launch just as it was about to pull out. 'I need to get out to the island – can I come aboard – I'll make it worth your while?' The dark blue fifty dollar note was all the convincing the boatman needed.

Billy stepped aboard, stumbling on the greasy boards and acting like a stupid tourist who'd suddenly decided to visit Tioman at night. The boatman was not bothered about Billy's motive; he had his fifty dollars and was thinking about the short trip out and the two passengers he was bringing back. If he'd turned round, he would have seen Billy crouching out of sight. The bumbling tourist, primed for danger, gripping the handle of his revolver. Billy was sure something really bad had happened to Alan and Barry – he just didn't know what. Billy's sixth sense was screaming a red alert warning.

Lee and Jannah had agreed their next move. The big city called: Singapore. Jannah longed to go shopping, to browse the counters at C.K. Tangs, get some new outfits and sexy underwear. She was desperate for new cosmetics. In her mind the list grew and grew ending with an almost physical ache for a pair of red high heels.

They'd lose themselves in the crowds and go to restaurants down Orchard Road. They would gorge themselves at Makan food stalls and drink ice-cold Tiger beer. They would take long hot showers. They would sleep forever on soft beds with clean sheets. They'd be together. They'd go to the cinema, go dancing and maybe see a band. They would be safe. They would recharge and recover.

Their new life would start with this short boat trip. They hugged each other as a blinking lantern became brighter and brighter as the launch approached the beach. They returned the skipper's friendly wave.

Billy moved with the lightness and grace of a gymnast. He slipped into the water over the side of the boat, hardly making a ripple, as the hull nudged the sand. He crouched waist deep waiting for the right moment to make his appearance. Above him, Lee caught a landing rope. Jannah stood behind Lee her hands full of bags and belongings. She froze as Billy rose from the waves, revolver in hand. His voice was clear and business-like.

'Now everyone, stay where you are. Don't make any sudden moves as I'm feeling a little nervous, and this gun has a hair trigger. We wouldn't want your lovely day trip to end in a nasty accident, would we?'

Inwardly, Lee and Jannah could not believe their foolishness. How could they have forgotten their training? Why did they let their guard down? They did as they were told, giving time for the shock to ease and their brains to work.

'I'm looking for two contacts of mine, two British soldiers. I don't suppose you've seen them?' Billy studied their faces for any reaction.

Jannah clicked into little girl mode. 'So sorry, my boyfriend and I came out this afternoon and we've been, well you know, we haven't seen each other for a long time and we've kept ourselves to ourselves – if you know what I mean. Perhaps they left earlier there are boats going back all day long, so sorry.' Lee was constantly amazed at Jannah's acting ability to become a completely different person in a blink of an eye.

Billy started to have doubts. His training led him to expect male adversaries, not a teenage couple on an island love trip. He lowered the pistol. 'Okay, I guess I need to take a look around. You don't mind waiting for a few minutes, I need to see if there's any sign of them?' Billy began calling and searching.

'Sure.' Lee spoke for the first time. While his face smiled, his eyes flashed a warning to Jannah. The telltale rifles stuck out from a blanket on the beach. With Billy looking the other way, Jannah and Lee scooped them up.

Billy swung round to see two Lee Enfield rifles trained upon him. He braced himself for death, said farewell to his loved ones in his head and made his peace with his God. A crushing blow from behind smashed him into unconsciousness. Goh Cheng, their communist contact and ferry boat skipper, held a hefty club in his hand. Billy's inert body lay at his feet.

'Let's go. Leave him. Tioman has seen enough blood for one day. Singapore is calling.' Jannah was already climbing into the boat.

A new world waited.

TWO

Five Years Later. 2nd February 1965. Chinese New Year – The Year of the Snake. Singapore.

'Ladies and gentlemen: Would you please extinguish cigarettes, fold your trays away, put your seats in an upright position and fasten your seat belts. We're in the final minutes of our descent into Paya Lebar International Airport. Tonight in Singapore, the Chinese New Year celebrations are in full swing. If you look out the cabin windows, you'll see some fabulous fireworks to welcome in the New Year.'

First time tourists went into ooh!-aah! mode and pointed to the flashing white lights that marked their descent with excitement in their eyes. The old hands knew better. The flight crew kept their nerve, and the Boeing 707, with its characteristic flapping wings, on a level approach. Tracer bullets fired from the Riau Islands zinged skyward, aiming to shoot down this international airliner. Never before had a BOAC stewardess needed a British stiff upper-lip.

Welcome to Singapore, welcome to the Indonesian Confrontation. A war so small, that hardly anyone in the world noticed.

***

Squadron Leader Peter Blake and family had arrived the same evening. They'd flown in to RAF Changi on a VC10 after a twenty-four hour flight, refuelling at Akrotiri in Cyprus, then on to the tiny island of Gan in the Maldives and finally onward to the heat and cloying humidity of Singapore. They reached the Katong Grange Hotel on the Singapore harbour waterfront late that night and fell into a soundless sleep. The next morning, Peter Blake left early to take up his duties at FEAFOC: Far East Air Force Operations Command.

FEAFOC was a central intelligence hub, strategically positioned in Singapore, the crossroads to the Far East. The western powers were fighting the spread of communism on two fronts in Vietnam and Indonesia. The Indonesian confrontation began in 1964. General Sukarno was attempting to annexe the northern Borneo states of Sabah and Sarawak that were part of Malaysia. As part of his campaign, Sukarno was launching insurgency attacks on mainland Malaya and Singapore.

The Ops Room never slept. The air conditioning was on full blast keeping the men and women of the morning watch cool in the furnace of activity. Day and night messages arrived and were decoded. The aim was to break the Indonesian army signal intercepts. The place hummed with radio static. Air traffic control screens scanned the area and radar sweeps checked shipping movements in the Singapore and Johor Straits.

Singapore was an island fortress with RAF air bases at Seletar and Tengah as well as Changi. The Royal Navy shipyard was at Sembawang in the north east of the island and the British army were in barracks at various locations including Gillman, Nee Soon and Alexandra. The sheer size and capability of these military assets acted as a deterrent to an all-out attack.

Meanwhile, back at the hotel, Blake's family slept on, got up, showered and went down to breakfast.

'Boiled egg, scrambled egg, toast, cereal, fresh orange. Tea and coffee if you're a grown-up. That's it.' Fourteen year old Chris Blake, still half asleep was not impressed with the breakfast menu. No fried egg. No sausages. No bacon. No fried bread. No H.P. sauce. His big sister Debbie seemed to accept it and reached for a slice of toast. Lily their mother, poured tea and smiled a serene smile and nodded a nod of acceptance as if to say: 'Children don't fuss, we're not in England now. We'll just have to get used to these ways and be more understanding and accepting'.

From their table they looked straight through the colonial style French windows onto the placid lawn dotted with towering palms. Anchored merchant vessels glittered in the morning sunlight. Chinese junks and sampans skittered back and forth like insects on a Far East pond. A peaceful riot of daily commerce had begun.

'BOMB! GET OUT NOW! EVERYONE OUT! NOW!' Chairs flung back, tea cups smashed, boiled eggs and toast crushed underfoot as twenty people leapt for the door, storming like a herd of chaotic Wildebeest, up the gravel drive to the welcoming safety of a police cordon, sprinting from peace to panic in one second flat.

At exactly the same moment, Peter Blake, dressed in his tropical uniform of desert boots, khaki shorts and short sleeved shirt, was about to enter the operations room to assume his intelligence duties. His superior officer acknowledged his arrival by raising a hand that signalled Stop and Hallo at one and the same time.

'Blake! There you are. Can't stop now – terrorist attack last night, bombs along the sea wall of Singapore harbour – sorting out the Singapore Defence Force and getting our bomb squad down there fast, speak in a moment.'

'Sir, whereabouts? My family are at a hotel by the harbour.'

'The Katong Grange Hotel.'

***

Lee Jaya, Jannah's partner, joined the Police safety cordon at the Katong Grange Hotel.

He calmly watched the bomb disposal crew go about their business. He waited for the bomb timers to explode. 'Anytime now,' he thought.

Lily, Debbie and Chris were also looking at their watches and moved away from the cordon to meet the school bus. Lee was not the only interested observer. Freddie Burton was in civilian clothes. He mingled with the crowd, missing nothing, looking for anyone or anything out of place. In all respects another innocent civilian - another innocent MI6 undercover agent.

Corporal Smyth had been on the booze the night before and was feeling the effects of too many vodka shots. He was first on the scene and saw three rusted OXO tins hanging from the edge of the sea wall. The insurgents had made a silly mistake; the bombs were all strung to be out of sight, but being low made them vulnerable to waves created by the wash of boats plying back and forth, letting water wash over the homemade bombs in their leaky tins.

This realisation relaxed Paddy Smyth. From a distance, his sergeant watched Paddy as he lifted the first tin, as gently as a new born babe. The lid came away to reveal three sticks of dynamite, a bedside alarm clock, still ticking, red and black cables menacingly connected. Two other colleagues had the lids off the remaining bombs and were making them safe, cutting the wires and removing the timers. They both raised their arms, shouting 'Clear!'

Paddy had pushed his luck on several occasions; getting a buzz from the danger. Usually his naturally sharp reactions outsmarted these little angels of death. Not now. His fuzzy brain heard a single clock click magnified a thousand times. Life left his body in a fireball.

***

Debbie and Chris saw their mum waving a motherly goodbye as they stared beyond her to the black and explosive cloud thrown in the air behind her. They saw Lily suddenly crouch down holding her head, then thankfully, slowly standing again. The Gharry bus kept going with its precious cargo of school children, up the East Coast Road, through the Siglap Gap and onto the Upper Changi Road.

Freddie's attention was on helping the injured and staying until a screaming ambulance arrived. Lily took a phone call and told Peter everything was under control. The hotel was undamaged, as the blast was at the far end of the breakwater. She and all the other guests owed a debt of thanks to Paddy Smyth. His body absorbed and stifled the blast. Lee slipped away unseen.

***

Debbie was wearing her mid-blue school dress with a white collar. She was slightly apprehensive but not overawed by the idea of joining the Lower Sixth in a co-educational school. Chris, being two years younger was the total opposite, being painfully shy and only used to a boys' school. Before the family left the UK, he'd been taken to Gamages in Oxford Street to their school outfitting department. As a result Chris was in abject misery. He had a new boy leather satchel by his side and a mercilessly short haircut, making his ears stick out like Dumbo the Elephant. His long khaki shorts made his legs look as though they were jammed inside two cornflake boxes. He knew beyond all doubt that today he would be chided, ridiculed and sport for all his classmates.

The other boys looked so comfortable and relaxed in tailored uniforms. Their shirts were soft cotton, some with epaulettes some without, some with breast pockets, some without. Shorts were short, styled and well fitted. These were the product of local tailors who could turn out a comfortable outfit inside a week for just a few dollars.

He decided to take his mind off these depressing thoughts by losing himself in the surroundings. This was his first day in a country that would shape the rest of his life. Bustling energy radiated everywhere.

Bright banners and posters in Chinese hung above the road or were pasted on telephone poles or the sides of buildings. Street hawkers selling all kinds of exotic foods dodged oncoming traffic in a daily game of chance. Chris noticed the metre wide monsoon drains, clogged with rubbish. Smells squirted into the bus; one moment the sweet tang of Satay sauce cooking on a giant wok, the next, the stomach churning stench from the open drains.

Ornamental Chinese, Buddhist and classical Muslim temples sat next to sombre Christian churches. They left built-up urban areas with concrete buildings to drive by Malay kampong villages. These were scenes of a crowded jumble of shanty huts, some lifted on wooden stilts to keep clear of monsoon floods. The hut walls made from Attap palm with rusted roofs of overlapping metal sheets. The kampong had only one water tap for drinking and washing. Dogs, chickens and pigs wandered in the mud, as if they had all the time in the world. Which in their world, they did.

As newcomers, Debbie and Chris were shown to their classes by the Head Boy and Head Girl. Debbie disappeared to the top floor in the L-shaped building. Chris walked along the ground floor corridor to 3A, the lowest ability streamed class.

'Find yourself an empty desk, anywhere will do.' His form teacher smiled. 'Everyone, this is Chris Blake, he'll be joining us. Please make him feel at home'.

Chris slid into the nearest desk to avoid walking any further than was necessary with all eyes on him. Thankfully, the eyes quickly lost interest in him. They were all looking out the window as two girls caught in a monsoon downpour ran across from the art block.

Helen Kensit and Cheryl Williams wiped the rain from their faces as they fell giggling through the classroom door.

'Sorry we're late sir!' They chimed in unison desperately trying to stifle laughter.

Chris had never seen anything like it. The girls were wearing the school uniform of white blouses with brown and white gingham skirts. Chris was in sensory overload. Their soaking wet blouses were transparent. Fabric stretched over curves that Chris had never witnessed before. He sat rigid, entranced, blinking in glorious shock. He could get used to this co-ed schooling idea.

'Girls, I think you'd better go and put your gym tops on, or the boys will never get any work done.'

THREE

2 Weeks Later. 16th February 1965 Singapore. The Rolling Stones last gig on their first Far East Tour.

Freddie Burton was meditating. He sat in a comfortable rattan armchair puffed with cushions on the upper deck of the Fairy Point Officer's Club, in the secure FEAFOC military compound, overlooking the lazy waters of the Johor Straits. He was using the technique of zonal focusing to relax, refresh and reboot his brain. He started by directing all his powers of concentration on his toes, wiggling them and feeling their existence at the far end of his physical consciousness. Then to his ankles, calves, knees, thighs, elbows and upward to the top of his head making sure that he gave respect and attention to every single part of his body in turn. He completed this mental sequence and while still in deep thought, turned his mind to the pack of photos lying on the table. The photos were the ones he'd taken at the Katong Grange Hotel bombing

The pictures were nagging him. No matter how many times he looked at them he knew something was missing. There were shots of the bomb disposal crew arriving and getting to work, pictures of the hotel guests holding each other and looking scared, pictures of one family with two kids in school uniform turning to leave the cordon and pictures of random onlookers who came to gawk. A picture of a lean, smart looking guy with a scar on his left check. The bystanders made up the majority of the photos. Freddie was wondering if he recognised anyone.

Then he saw it. Five dots. Five dots tattooed on the knuckle of a ring finger on the left hand of a young Chinese man, the mark of a Triad gang member. The dots called Tiams show the status of the fighter or enforcer. The youth had an extra teardrop tattoo on his cheek to signify the death of a fellow gang member. These identification marks were like having a neon sign flashing his allegiance. Freddie's brain was troubled. 'What was a member of the criminal underworld doing there?'

Freddie was Eurasian of mixed blood with a Malay mother and English father. He had talents that were perfectly suited to his MI6 cover. Acting was second nature. He had the gift of being able to change his appearance in the blink of an eye. His ability to speak Malay and Mandarin would see him equally invisible in Chinatown, in a Malay kampong shack, or sitting quietly sipping fresh lime juice sweetened with sugar and served with crushed ice as a British officer. Freddie could alter his appearance to match the environment. He was a human chameleon, never standing out, always blending in. Whatever role he chose, you would never guess at his intense fitness, unarmed combat skills and martial arts training. Overall his greatest asset was in the top three inches of his head. His brain was a deadly weapon.

***

'Freddie! Sorry I'm late, more problems in Saigon.' Cody Jackson, Freddie's opposite number in the CIA, shattered his quiet contemplation with all the tact, style and sensitivity of a baby rhino. 'Fresh lime, please.' Cody gave his order to the Chinese waiter with an abruptness of someone used to being obeyed. He got straight down to business. 'I need your inside knowledge with a little matter concerning our Red friends. I've been told you're the man with eyes and ears everywhere on this little Island.'

Freddie had read Cody's file prior to this first meeting. Despite his crass arrogance, Cody was a cunning and subtle operator. Freddie wasn't fooled by the performance he'd just witnessed. He knew Cody had been chosen to lead the CIA operations against Sukarno and warranted respect, at least until proven otherwise. Game playing was second nature to Cody and in Freddie, he'd found a fellow player.

'What's on your mind?' Freddie pushed forward his first metaphorical pawn on the chess board of subversion.

'Oleg Rozanov. Have you heard of him?' Cody continued, not waiting nor expecting an answer. 'He's yet another economic attaché to join the Soviet Consulate in Singapore. What he knows about grain yields in the Ukraine wouldn't fill a postage stamp, he's KGB. That's the bad news. This is the good news. This is his first trip outside Russia and his first exposure to the delights of the Orient. That's where you come in. My bosses in Langley would like to set an irresistible honey trap for Oleg. We want him to be the star of his own adult movie. Can you spin a web of irresistible sexual attraction to snare our Oleg?'

'Tools of the trade.' Freddie answered in the affirmative and continued. 'To be really effective we need to know what perversion presses his button.' Freddie was warming to the challenge. 'It could be straight sex, or he may have a kinky deviant fetish, bondage, sado-masochism or something we haven't even thought of yet. Who knows, he may have a foot fetish, Oleg could be a toe sucker!' Freddie and Cody spilled their drinks in spasms of snorting laughter.

Recovering, Freddie decided: 'This calls for a trip to Bugis Street.'

'Bugis Street?' Cody was all attention and anticipation.

Freddie explained. 'That's the place and I've got just the girl for the job. She's an expert at pushing buttons. She'll be our agent of extreme pleasure for Comrade Rozanov; he won't know what's hit him.' Freddie needed more background. 'I've got a feeling you're not telling me everything; if we're to work together I need to know what's really going on, these days knowledge saves lives – and that means my life.'

Cody gathered his thoughts. 'What do you see from this balcony?' Cody continued without pause. 'The Johor Straits, they're a vital link from the sea to the naval base. The Straits are narrow and ships have barely enough water to clear their hulls. Submarines ride on the surface because it's so shallow. These waters are a prime target for the Indonesians to sow mines.'

Freddie was waiting for Cody to get to the point as he already knew this.

'Our Mister Rozanov's real job is naval affairs. The Russians sold various warships to the Indonesians in 1962, including Jaguar motor torpedo boats and submarines. We know the Soviets have been involved in training and Russian sailors are manning their M-Class diesel/electric submarine fleet. We need to get better intelligence on their movements and any threat of an Indonesian invasion. By compromising Oleg, we'll be able to apply pressure to get that vital information.

That's why I've been sent to Singapore to take a more offensive route, by either overt or covert means. That's where you come in.'

'Covert is good.' Freddie had an inkling of a plan. 'I'll meet you in Changi Village at nine tonight. The Amah's market is on a Tuesday evening. Leave your Hawaiian shirt and Bermuda shorts behind. Blending in is the name of the game. We'll share a pick-up taxi into town. See you at nine by Joe's Place; it's a coffee stall half way up on the right hand side. You should try their instant coffee with condensed milk - it'll be a rare experience for an American.'

Freddie left. He had calls to make, things to arrange.

***

Chris had to pinch himself. Only a few weeks before he had been frozen, soaked from head to foot, his Mirror sailing dinghy having capsized in the River Orwell in Ipswich. He was crewing and the supposedly experienced helm failed to ease the mainsheet as a strong gust caught them. The main sail acted like a solid door as the wind hit it and the boat flipped right over. That was bad enough, but the river was swarming with jelly fish which totally freaked the helmsman.

The jelly fish were slipping, sliding, stinging, as their tentacles stung faces, hands and legs. The upturned dinghy was carried down the river with the boys hanging on for dear life. It took forty freezing minutes for the rescue boat to reach them and tow them back against the current.

Today, his feet were dangling in warm water, the sun on his face, in paradise. Chris and Kobz were sitting on the pontoon at Changi Yacht Club.

'Oh! Paul, do yah wanna' hold my hand? John, a kiss on the lips, please, please me! Oh! Ringo, my friend fancies you! George, do you want to touch my little titties?'

The boys were helpless with laughter, sending up all the girls in the class with their infatuation with The Beatles. They put on girly voices and did hilarious movements with hips, lips and hands to match their awful impressions.

They were larking about to cover their disappointment as they had no chance of seeing The Rolling Stones playing at the Badminton Hall. It was to be their last gig in Singapore at the end of their first Far East Tour.

Kobz had to return to their disappointment. 'Dave Tommo has bunked off school to take some pictures. They've been seen sunbathing by the Hilton pool. Brian Jones, Charlie Watts and Keith Richards were lounging around, no sign of Mick and Bill. You should have seen the newspaper: the advert called them 'The Wild Men from Richmond!'

Freddie had been listening to their banter. He'd walked along the wooded path from the Officer's Club, pass the Padang and along to the yacht club.

He owned Galadriel, a beautiful teak sailing yacht moored off the beach.

'Thirty five shows, sixteen venues all over Australia, tonight will be the last before flying back to England. Sorry guys, I overheard you talking about The Stones. Such a pity you won't be going.' Chris and Kobz turned to see Freddie standing on the higher jetty, looking down and speaking to them as if they were real people and not annoying little kids.

'You know The Stones were on Shindig, the American TV show, two days before they flew out to begin their Far East Tour? Man, they must be exhausted.' The boys looked at each other. They knew Freddie as a club member but had not spoken to him before.

Freddie continued. 'Apparently they're going to be playing all their new stuff, Not Fade Away, The Last Time, Can't get no satisfaction, I'm a King Bee. Such a pity you won't be there, a real pity.'

Freddie left that disastrous thought hanging long enough for their misery to assume epic proportions. He spoke again as if a new idea had suddenly popped into his head; which of course, it hadn't. 'There's just one thing, I'm looking for. A couple of boys to help me out from time to time, cleaning Galadriel and running a few errands. These will be paid jobs, a bit of pocket money. I don't suppose you know of anyone?'

Kobz and Chris were on their feet before Freddie reached the question mark. 'Okay, it's a deal then. Trust is at the heart of our arrangement. What we do is between the three of us, no parents, no other friends or adults must know. Understood?' An excited 'Yes' clinched the contract.

'As it turns out I've got a meeting tonight, I won't make the Badminton Hall. Do you know anyone who'd like these two tickets? They're for some band called The Rolling Stones.'

The whoops of joy echoed across the water.

The boys were becoming fast friends. Chris remembered how they met. On Chris's first day (the day Helen Kensit was burned into his memory forever), he was standing dressed in his sports kit, nervous about joining a group standing by a massive monsoon puddle. They waved Chris over. 'Grab a leg, arm, anything!' They were in a circle lifting a struggling victim high in the air.

The cry went up 'Run!' The group picked up speed with the boy dangling between them as they got closer and closer to the puddle. 'Now!' The victim was launched like a skipping stone and landed in a huge spray of water, mud and grass. The group quickly disbanded and began practising their 'Not me Sir' excuses. Chris stared down at the piece of human wreckage that shook himself rising from the puddle, spitting out a mouthful of grass. Smiling as he spoke, 'HI! I'm Kobz'.

Children in the ground floor classrooms were standing, shouting and cheering at the scene. Tom Hollamby, the most feared teacher in the school, blew his whistle.

'You two: Detention!' The first of many. Their friendship lasted decades.

***

February weather in Preston and Oldham was as different from the tropics as it is possible to get. Two postmen, both shielding their postbags from the bitter driving rain, leaned their bicycles against dirty walls in grimy streets of terraced houses, to deliver two identical brown envelopes. The envelopes fell to doormats with bills and rent demands. These were put to one side to be ignored, until they couldn't be ignored any longer.

The brown envelopes bearing a British Army postmark contained identical letters bearing an identical message. The only difference was that one was addressed to the next of kin of Rifleman Alan Jenkins, and the other to Private Barry Snell.

The letters read:

> It is with great regret that the time has come to close our files on the disappearance of your son on or around 30th July 1960, in the Malayan jungle. Despite exhaustive enquiries over the last five years, we have not been able to find any trace of his whereabouts.
>
> Therefore, following standard procedure, your son has been officially classified as missing in action and believed to be dead.
>
> Following receipt of this letter you can now claim the Army support allowance. A claim form is included.
>
> From our records, we know your son served his country valiantly, displaying conduct above the call of duty.
>
> Yours sincerely
>
> **Major N. Metcalf**
> Army Family Liaison Officer

***

When members of the Armed Forces arrive in Singapore they're given an 'Out of Bounds' book. This is to reduce any chance of friction between misbehaving troops and the local population. The book, as the title suggests, lists trouble spots to be avoided by the military. Armed with this vital piece of information, troops learned exactly where to go to have a good time. Bugis Street was top of the list.

Cody and Freddie left the pick-up taxi and crossed the footbridge near Change Alley and made their way through winding streets and jostling crowds. They felt at ease. Singapore was a melting pot of races, each allowing the others to do their own thing, well, most of the time.

During the daytime Bugis Street was just like any other. Shops showcased the riches of the orient alongside grocery stalls, souvenir shops and eating places. In the apothecary you could buy Chinese medicines and potions for every malady known to man, from hair loss to impotency to aphrodisiacs. The dusty windows held bulbous glass jars with snakes, monkeys and other creatures of the jungle preserved in formaldehyde.

If you walked through the ancient carved wooden doorway it was like stepping back a hundred years. The air inside never moved. It had a silent presence to match the attentive Taoist physician, who enquired about the celestial balance of your 'Chi'. He would reach for the mortar and pestle for herbs taken from a wall full of symmetrical drawers to concoct a powder to cure practically any ailment.

When night fell, Bugis Street was dedicated to earthly delights. All senses and sensations satisfied.

Round wooden pavement tables, chairs and stools were scattered outside Indian, Malay and Chinese restaurants. The tantalising aromas of Szechuan and Cantonese dishes mingled in the evening air with Malaysian and Indian food, all fighting to stimulate taste buds and deliciously satisfy appetites.

Freddie chose Cantonese and ordered two Tiger beers and Dim Sum. He loved the heavenly bite-sized parcels of dumplings with a variety of fillings, steamed and served in round bamboo baskets. Freddie decided to take it slow and give Cody's palate time to graduate from T-bone steaks smothered in barbeque sauce.

Dish followed dish, Tiger followed Tiger. By 10.30pm they were ready for business, ready to play the game of entrapment and meet Freddie's mysterious contact.

'Cody, what you're about to witness must stay with you alone, never to be revealed to anyone. Failure to keep this pact will jeopardise years of work and destroy contacts in the Singapore underworld for good.'

Freddie was taking a risk, but knew that ultimately Cody would be floating in the Singapore River to pay the price for any duplicity. He read Cody's response in his eyes and was satisfied the calculated risk would play to his advantage. One thing that Freddie had learned early in his career: you should always hedge your bets. Eyes that aren't meant to lie often do.

'There's just one thing. You'll have to wear these.' Freddie drew a pair of sunglasses from his jacket pocket. 'These have a special feature, they have solid black lenses; you won't be able to see a thing. It's better than making you wear a blindfold. People will think you are either a tourist or a blind man. It's a request from my contacts who are nervous of meeting someone for the first time, you understand.' Cody slipped them on and gripped Freddie's forearm. He played a blind man.

There was method in Freddie's madness. He'd taken the meal at a leisurely pace. The later it got, the more people were moving up and down the street, voices grew louder and noise levels double, making it more difficult for Cody to know where he was going amid the seething hustle and bustle.

They stopped by an ornately carved wooden door, lined on the inside with steel. A glass peep-hole was cut into the eye of a fearsome dragon. A single human eyeball looked out, recognised Freddie and slipped the lock. The huge door swung open soundlessly, just wide enough to enter and shut immediately. Cody's sense of smell detected deep notes of resin countered with the floral lightness of frangipani and orchid; the unmistakable aroma of opium.

Freddie removed Cody's glasses. They were alone, in a place of utter tranquillity. The blissful sound of a Guqin, the classical seven-stringed Chinese zither, was being played somewhere in the background. The sound of such gentleness was completely soundproofed from the riotous noise of the street outside.

They stood in a luxurious atrium with a circular glass roof; three ceiling fans stepped at different heights stirred the cooling air. Huge carp swam languidly under a miniature curved bridge over a pond. An imposingly large statue of Guan Yu, the Chinese God of War, straddled the pond. The statue was a potent symbol of power and a reminder not to act inappropriately in this pleasure palace.

Red and gold banners decorated with scenes from mythology with beautifully embroidered images of dragons, warriors and beautiful maidens hung from ceiling to floor. Eight doors were embedded in the walls of the atrium leading to private chambers. A hostess appeared from nowhere wearing a scarlet cheongsam embroidered with swirls of sparkling gold, picked out with silver thread, that melded erotically to every curve of her body.

She motioned them to follow as she walked straight into a wall. Seconds before making contact, the wall slid sideways to reveal a spiral staircase leading underground to a sumptuous high class bordello. The door slid back into position as if pulled by invisible strings. Cody was stupefied. He was expecting the expected; a low rent oriental brothel.

Not this sophisticated, luxurious, temple of erotica. The hostess continued her conducted tour. The walls held paintings from the Perfumed Garden, cushioned booths with privacy drapes were cradled in subdued lighting. A champagne bar, better than any luxury hotel, displayed a choice of Möet et Chandon, Veuve Clicquot, Laurent Perrier to suit the many preferences of their discerning clientele. The hostess moved with deft little steps, seeming to float past a succession of private chambers. She introduced each one in turn.

'This one is for our guests who relish the attentions of our oriental temptresses, this one for our beautiful girls from the subcontinent, experts in the Kama

Sutra, and here is our bondage chamber of pain with exhibition seating for voyeurs, and last, our steam baths with massage beds. Whatever your pleasure, whatever your desire, we live to serve. Please take a seat at the champagne bar, our honourable madam, Tiger Mother, will be with you in a moment.'

The most beautiful woman Cody had ever seen stepped through a curtain of finest silk. She was the living embodiment of a modern day Mata Hari. The vision wore a headdress of pearl beads, cascading diamond earrings and a necklace of precious gems. Pearls decorated a black basque, her gently heaving breasts swelling with each breath. She wore stockings and suspenders with red high heeled stilettos under a transparent jade silk sarong.

Cody was transfixed. His temperature shot skyward. His brain sent blood gushing southward. She stood, knowing and relishing the primal erotic power she wielded.

Freddie spoke four words very slowly.

'Cody, this is Jannah.'

FOUR

3 Weeks later. Wednesday 10th March 1965. MacDonald House Bombing, Singapore.

Kobz was getting frustrated. His pupil had two left feet. 'Let's try again. The step-over is a simple dance; the basics first. The left leg steps over the right, the right leg slips backwards. As this is happening, bounce on the balls of your feet and repeat the action. Your arms move with your swaying hips, repeat and repeat. What's so difficult?'

'It's okay for you but the messages from my brain get lost round my ankles!' Chris wanted to call it a day. He was changing fast, hair longer, new school uniform, cornflake box shorts thrown in the rubbish. All he needed was to master the dance moves for the step-over and he'd be ready for Seletar Youth Club at the weekend. The boys had met Katie Baker and Libby Stewart, schoolmates from Changi Grammar, at the Rolling Stones gig.

Kobz was sure that there was more than a flicker of interest from Katie. He was smitten with her cute freckles and big brown eyes. He needed Chris to learn the step-over so his crafty plan would work. Chris was to be his wingman while he lured Katie away from her friends, who would be dancing round an impenetrable ring of handbags on the floor. The girls danced close together forming a defensive line against unwanted boy attacks. Once he'd got Katie on her own, he could try out a few devastating chat-up lines, only he had none, all of his were cringe worthy.

The boys continued to practise their steps to the manic giggling of Kobz's two young sisters, hiding behind the lounge door. It didn't faze the boys. They knew they were irresistible to the opposite sex. They were both wearing their new outfits straight from Kiam Sing Tailors in Changi village. They wore red and yellow check shirts with quartered hipster trousers, the top quarters were swirling blue paisley and the bottom, small orange checks. They got admiring looks (some say astonished!) when they picked up their new avant-garde designs. They were heartbreakers. In not quite the words of The Kinks, they were dedicated followers of (their own) fashion. Girls would be putty in their hands. Such was the magnitude of their shared delusion.

It was all Freddie could do to keep a straight face as the boys walked down the pavement towards him. 'Guys! Looking good! Hot dates?' The boys mistook his grin for appreciation of their sense of style. 'I heard The Stones were amazing, and the girls were screaming the place down.'

The boys relived the gig, and bounced adjectives between them.

'Brilliant'

'Incredible'

'Amazing'

'Ace'

'N-Mega'

'Mega-Ace'

'Okay, so you liked it.' Freddie got the picture. 'You haven't forgotten our deal have you? I need an urgent letter delivered, and I can't it trust to the postman. Who would like to volunteer?'

'Me' Chris held out his hand and took a plain white envelope. Nothing was written on it, no name, no address, only five dots in a square pattern with a dot at each corner and one in the middle.

'And me.' Kobz leapt in, no way was he going to be left out. The boys couldn't wait to take on this secret mission, especially as they had a rare afternoon off school.

'Right, this is what I want you to do. Go to the cinema and have a good time.' Two sets of boy's eyebrows shot upwards. Dr Terror's House of Horrors, starring Christopher Lee and Peter Cushing, is showing at the Lido Cinema in Orchard Road. The afternoon screening starts at 3 o'clock. Simply go to the box office, ask for two tickets and hand them this envelope. The attendant will give you your tickets – no money will change hands. Here's ten dollars for the pick-up taxi, coke and ice cream. See you back here at Joe's around 7pm.'

It was 2.15 pm when the boys decided to take the bus and pocket the taxi fare. They couldn't believe their luck.

***

At precisely 3.07pm a bomb exploded by the lift on the mezzanine floor of the Hong Kong and Shanghai Bank building, Orchard Road.

Mrs Suzie Choo 36, private secretary to the Bank Manager and Miss Juliet Goh 23, a filing clerk, were killed instantly. Thirty-three people were injured. The bomb, placed by two Indonesian saboteurs, smashed the lift door. Another connecting door was blown apart. Glass from shattered windows rained down upon passing traffic and pedestrians. Exploding glass does not discriminate. Glass hurtled through the humid air, slicing and cutting skin and bone. The shock wave blew riders from their mopeds. Cars and trucks swerved and crashed in a slow motion ballet of destruction.

This was the twenty-ninth bomb attack in Singapore since the beginning of the Indonesian Confrontation.

With so many heavily defended military bases in Singapore, teams of agent provocateurs concentrated on soft civilian targets. This would go hand-in-hand with sowing discontent among the population with two aims. One was to get the population to rise up against their colonial masters. The second was to turn community against community, creed against creed, Asian and Malay against the dominant Chinese to instigate race riots and destabilise the ebb and flow of normal life.

What's normal to the criminal underworld is another matter. Members of street gangs were loyal to their brotherhood and were protective of their territory, their gambling and opium dens, their whore houses and protection rackets.

But they were Singaporeans. The Indonesian saboteurs were outsiders, a new and unwelcome gang in town. These repeated bombings were bad for business.

Something had to be done.

***

Oleg Rozanov chaired his weekly review meeting in the basement of the Russian consulate. The stenographer took notes. His hand-picked team of field operatives and logistics personnel made their progress reports. 'I'd like to welcome Captain Hakim of the Indonesian Marine Corps who, as they say, is on a flying visit to Singapore.' Oleg injected this levity as Hakim had been smuggled onto the Island undercover and would be transported back to his base in Bantam within the hour, aboard a boat waiting in Keppel Harbour.

'Captain Hakim is here to brief us on requirements for the next phase of the naval campaign and to confirm acceptance of two Whiskey Class submarines, as a gift from our glorious Soviet Pacific Fleet. Lastly, I would like him to pass on our congratulations for the recent insurgent activities. Especially the explosion today.' They clapped until their palms glowed red.

'It's unfortunate that Captain Hakim has to leave, as tonight you're all invited to celebrate today's brave strike against capitalism.'

***

Chris and Kobz were glued to the screen, mouths opened in awe as they watched the 'Coming Soon' trailer for Thunderball, the fourth James Bond film due for release later in the year. Sean Connery was whizzing through the air wearing an incredible jetpack, driving an Aston Martin DB5 like a mad man, and fighting the evil SMERSH underwater - all the while avoiding bigger and bigger explosions.

The onscreen explosions were as loud as the devastation taking place at the MacDonald Building in Orchard Road.

They didn't hear it as they were cradled in the soundproofed, womb-like darkness of the cinema, slurping coke through straws and speed-eating popcorn. Dr Terror's House of Horrors gave them a gruesome diet of vampires, disembodied hands, werewolves and voodoo – delicious. They loved it. The real horror outside was completely lost on them.

'My God!' Freddie's hand squeezed the telephone so hard that it would have snapped clean in two if it hadn't been made from solid Bakelite. His controller broke the news about the Orchard Road bombing. Freddie's 'My God!' was followed by 'Fuck!' as he realised the boys could be caught in the blast.

Luckily the Macdonald building was further along Orchard Road, so by the time the credits rolled on Dr Terror's House of Horrors, ambulances and fire engines had arrived and the station wagon that belonged to the Australian High Commission had been removed from the central divide, where it was blown in the blast. Traffic was moving normally again.

The boys ran to catch the Changi bus. They sprinted out of the Lido to the bus station without a backward glance. The two English kids roamed freely in this bustling, oriental city without a worry. That's just the way it was. They felt safe in Singapore.

Even though they'd arranged to meet at 7pm, Freddie had been sitting at Joe's since six. He was smoking to find a way to lessen his manic anxiety and stubbing out cigarette after cigarette. He needed to do something with his hands while anxiously waiting as bus after bus arrived without the boys.

At last they turned up and totally oblivious to what had happened in Orchard Road, the two were mock fighting, SMERSH against 007. Unaware of the real life secret agent, sitting across the road and stressed out of his mind.

**

Billy Chang was unwinding. His unit had returned to Singapore for a few days Rest and Recuperation, after night patrols in Borneo. He and a few mates had chosen Bugis Street for their R&R venue. Even though he'd had a few beers, Billy's sixth sense was totally sober, his memory as sharp as a blade. It still took him a while to place the man hovering by one of the market stalls. The man seemed to be on alert, scoping people coming and going, on sentry duty, keeping watch. The realisation came when Billy remembered staring down the barrel of a rifle on Tioman Island.

If Billy had been on full operational mode, he might have sprung into dynamic action. It was the ice in his soul that kept him cool, as he knew that drawing a weapon in a crowded city street was not the smartest idea. And anyway he had to keep things balanced and consider the Tioman incident from another viewpoint, another scenario.

What would he have done, if he had been enjoying a day on the beach with his girlfriend, who he hadn't seen for some time, then suddenly been threatened by a stranger armed with a revolver? There was no sign of Alan and Barry, and nothing to say these two lovers were in any way involved. Okay, they did have two Lee Enfield rifles but Malaya was awash with small arms, especially Lee Enfields. The skipper of their boat was obviously trying to protect them from a maniac. The blow to his head in the circumstances was not bad at all, he could be lying dead in the sand.

Billy involuntarily touched his head where the blow hit, then recognised a player in this drama who put his mind at ease. Freddie and Cody had slipped into a couple of chairs a few tables away. Billy had seen Freddie at one of the SAS briefing sessions and knew he was on their side. He saw a flicker of recognition between Freddie and the lookout, so something was going on, an operation was in play. A table of bawdy, drunken Russians, drinking vodka shots, was getting rowdy. The Russians were with a group of working girls laughing and teasing for later lust and money. The table was positioned close to a narrow alleyway.

Billy watched as two girls, one on each arm, guided a very drunken but very happy Russian, away from the table and disappear into the alley. A single human eyeball peered out from a fearsome dragon's eye and a lock released. Billy noticed that Freddie and Cody had disappeared on cue.

It was a single camera shoot with full audio and vision through a two-way mirror. Oleg lay naked on a massive bed surrounded by mirrors on walls and ceiling. He was receiving expert three-way attention that stoked his desire. The girls sensuously shed items of clothing like the seasoned actresses they were. Each piece removed with such style that Oleg lapped up the private dances these beautiful girls provided.

When the girls got down to their G-strings it didn't register that their womanly curves were far more pronounced, bigger bulges than expected. It was so wrong. As their wigs dropped to the floor, the Ladyboys of Bugis Street earned their fee with relish. Oleg surrendered to this wickedly exciting experience.

The camera kept rolling.

Freddie and Cody were primed and ready for blackmail.

FIVE

3 Days later. Friday 12th March 1965. After the bombing. Time to hatch a plan.

You could be forgiven for thinking Yip Chung Lau was eccentric. How many people do you know who on a whim, day or night, would change into the clothes of a street hawker then slip into traffic pedalling a rickshaw? Whatever the weather, monsoon or shine, he would become part of the Singapore scene picking up tourists or diplomats, high born or low, and take them through the dusty, dirty streets to their destinations for just a few dollars. You may think his behaviour was odd, incomprehensible, the product of a deranged mind. Here's some advice. Keep that thought silent – never, ever, speak it out loud.

The reason? Yip Chung Lau, also known as Jonny Lau, is the Dragon Head, the Mountain Master, the leader of the 6-6-6 Triad gang. The strategist and controller of the most feared criminal gang in Singapore. The 6-6-6 gang could trace its ancestry back to the Shaolin Buddhist warrior monks, famous for the development of the martial art of Kung Fu. The significance is the numbers added together total 18, to represent the 18 principal disciples of Shaolin. Jonny Lau, now in his early forties, was responsible for the rebirth of the 6-6-6 following the Japanese invasion in February 1942.

He was just 19 when the Japanese invaded. The victors herded young Chinese boys together and ordered them to form two parallel columns. Jonny stood shoulder to shoulder with his younger brother Kim. They stared into each other's eyes, sealing out the dread reality that surrounded them, they spoke their last goodbyes. Jonny's column survived. Kim met his death. An estimated 50,000 young Chinese men were shot, or bayonetted, to save ammunition, during the first days of Japanese occupation.

Survival spurred Jonny and the 6-6-6 to go to war against the Japanese, resisting their occupation at every turn. They were not alone. Members of other criminal gangs put their own disputes to one side and banded together against this common enemy, while maintaining their own business interests of narcotics, gambling, prostitution and protection. That rare alliance was over twenty years ago. Now, they were faced with another possible Indonesian invasion and a fresh challenge to their lucrative business interests.

The invisible spirit of his brother Kim rode for free in Jonny's rickshaw. Jonny shared his most secret plans with Kim; his most private and secure confidant. Sharing helped clarify schemes in his head as he roamed the streets keeping an expert eye on his territory, checking the loyalty of his minions and the infringements of rival gangs in the guise of a no-account rickshaw driver.

Tonight he needed to take to the streets for another reason. The message he received from Freddie, marked with the five Tiams, needed quality thinking time. It was a measure of Jonny's standing in the criminal fraternity that he could go wherever and whenever he wanted in Singapore. Other street gang leaders alerted their underlings on Jonny's rickshaw trips to make sure nothing bad happened to him. The repercussions would be too awful to contemplate; the start of a new turf war.

As Jonny's feet pushed the pedals, an idea, courtesy of Kim from the afterlife, came fully formed into his mind. The image of a gang map of Singapore crystallised in his mind. To the north, the Ang Soon Tong gang controlled the area from the 10 milestone and Pek Kim Seng controlled Bugis Street and Chinatown. Jonny worked through the geography of crime, ending with the Red Butterfly Gang; an all-girl gang who gave protection to female night club workers and bar girls operating in the Clifford Pier and Capitol Theatre area, to the south along the harbour.

Jonny's idea was rooted in the past but perfect for the future. He thanked Kim and turned for home.

***

Freddie watched her sleeping.

Jannah had sex. Freddie made love. Her tousled hair lay on the pillow like static waves in a silent storm, her breasts rising and falling in glorious rhythmic cadence, her perfect naked body bathing in the afterglow, sealed within a hollow of deep contentment.

It'd happened so fast. It wasn't meant to be.

'What have I done? How could I fall hopelessly in love? How could I become so vulnerable, so quickly?' Freddie's head had lost the battle with his heart. For years, through all his training, he'd locked his feelings inside a strongbox of emotional steel. Steel melted in seconds by the searing torch of desire. She was funny, intelligent, sexy off-the-scale.

She'd turned his life upside down and inside out.

***

Freddie was not the only male lost in the ways of women. Chris was the school boy willing to be schooled but didn't know where to start. That's why he'd signed up for an additional Biology lesson. Today's lesson was the one-handed brassiere release technique.

Kobz and Nick Shilling were giving Chris the theory before a practical session. The boys were sitting in classroom 3A during lunch break.

First things first. Nick asked the question – 'Are you left handed or right handed?'

'Left.' Chris checked to make sure.

'Right – no don't say - left – I know you meant left,' Nick was getting confused already. He continued.

'Stick out your thumb and forefinger of your left hand – good. Now curl the other three fingers under, this technique requires the action of the thumb and forefinger working together. Understand?' Chris was with him so far. 'What you are about to learn will show girls that you are experienced, a real man of the world!' Chris liked that.

Kobz joined the training session and spoke with the seriousness of the designer of the Atom Bomb. 'Bra clasps have two parts, but only one that moves. Are you with me Chris?' The eager student nodded.

'The two parts are called hooks and eyelets, and there are sets of either two or three rows in standard bra straps. Bikini tops are different with one hook, we'll come to that later. We need to concentrate on the standard contraption for now. We'll also discuss cup sizes but that's a more advanced level, we'll keep that for another day. Are you with me Chris?'

Nick rejoined the tutorial and took over. 'Now straighten your index finger like so.' Nick's finger was impressively straight and vertically pointed to the classroom ceiling. 'This finger is laid flat against the girls back on the row of brassiere eyes, understand?'

'Yes,' affirmed Chris with rapt attention.

'The second part of the movement is for the thumb to both squeeze and roll the hooks over the eye holes in a smooth twist of the wrist. Done smoothly, the bra strap will be released in one fluid movement. Chris was staring at his left hand thumb and finger practising the technique over and over again; this was worth doing the extra homework.

'Practice makes perfect,' Kobz intoned. 'Now for the practical lesson – anyone you want to go solo with on your practical?'

Chris had a dream-flash of Helen Kensit. He was momentarily lost running slow-motion through cornfields with Helen bra-less. He then snapped back to reality. She would have to wait until he could pluck up courage and become knowledgeable in the ways of the woman.

'How about Katie Baker?' Chris ventured, Kobz shot him a look of pure venom. 'How about Cheryl?' Chris was fresh out of human manikins.

Nick nodded. 'Yeah, she might co-operate in the spirit of advancing man's quest for knowledge.' Cheryl agreed and they set off to the sports field for the practical. Nick began the exercise with deft fingers. A first gentle press inwards against skin, a slight lifting of the bra catch and pressure from the thumb, twist, turn and free, with just one hand and one fluid movement. Cheryl had her arms crossed across her chest as the bra sprung free. A quick refastening then Kobz demonstrated his practised touch. It was now the turn of the novice.

Chris's nerves got the better of him. His mouth was dry and his heart beat faster, stress kicked in. His left hand, slowly, tentatively tried the thumb and forefinger twist in mid-air as final practice. He moved closer and closer to Cheryl's bra strap. He was certain he'd get an electric shock when his fingers touched, just inches now...

'You four - detention!'

Tom Hollamby's voice carried across the running track, a steely look in his eyes. The sound wave from his whistle reverberated in the accusing air.

***

Cody was having a hard time, getting chewed out, dragged over the carpet – you get the picture. Langley were delighted with the Oleg movie but wanted results to go with it. Cody needed to make it productive and fast.

Oleg was having a hard time at the same time. He was getting chewed out, dragged over the carpet by his superiors as well. Moscow wanted to see some positive results of his activities. As a new KGB operative he needed to demonstrate control and productive liaisons with the Indonesians, and some return on the free ordnance donated by the Soviet Socialist Republics. Oleg needed results and fast.

When he got back to his desk a brown envelope lay hidden under the morning mail, marked 'Personal & Private'. His normally florid complexion drained in an instant to the colour of milky grey porcelain. Forgotten memories of a night on the town, threatening black and white evidence captured in celluloid sprang from the envelope. Luckily, he was alone in his office holding the photo when his world stopped spinning. A slip of paper fell on the floor. It read: 'Tiger Balm Gardens by the laughing Buddha. 11 a.m. today. Be there.'

Cody was starting to get productive. He was offering Oleg a fair exchange between the negatives and information, the choice between a way out, and a one-way trip to the Gulag, between death and defection. He'd chosen the Tiger Balm Gardens, a busy tourist theme park, for this first meeting. The gardens were created by the Aw Brothers – Aw Boon Haw and Aw Boon Par, to represent scenes from ancient Chinese stories with fantastical statues and tableaux after making their fortunes from sales of their Tiger Balm ointment.

This time, Cody was wearing his Hawaiian shirt and looked every inch the American tourist, snapping everything that moved and volunteering to take photos for people as they grinned for the folks back home. He'd walked up the steps and through the entrance to the gardens which was in the form of a gigantic mouth of a dragon. Cody sauntered down the length of its tail before taking up his position to wait for Oleg. Cody was unarmed.

He took a pragmatic view of these encounters. Cody knew he had to allow time for Oleg's anger and embarrassment to subside and to concentrate on the upside. Gone were the days when he'd adopt an aggressive posture. He rather liked the idea that Oleg was a man of passion and able to enjoy himself, like he did. They both worked in the same game, both aware of the risks and both got high on danger. He'd caught Oleg red-handed (Cody chuckled at the pun) and needed to develop his asset and not alienate him. Because they were both working in subversion, Cody had spent time thinking about different scenarios to develop once Oleg realised he was between a rock and a hard place.

Sending coded reports containing valuable information was what Moscow expected to see. Cody had devised some high class misinformation that would keep Oleg in station and impress his masters. In return, Cody wanted more intelligence on Indonesian tactics, training bases and operations in Singapore. To sweeten the deal, he would hand Oleg a brown envelope bulging with dollars for his living expenses and discuss a possible exit strategy.

At the end of his usefulness in Singapore, Oleg could disappear into the CIA's Witness Protection Programme, absorbed and forgotten somewhere in the mid-west with a lovely wife, a lovely house and lovely children with perfect teeth. Cody would use Oleg's inexperience as his ace.

Oleg was armed. He anticipated ridicule. He expected gloating. He was certain of a world of pain, if he didn't co-operate. He was also smart enough to think of ways to turn this situation to his advantage. Perhaps he could identify key CIA agents. He may let the CIA think he was running scared and use this apparent weakness to deceive them. He could always use his contacts to arrange a killing or two. Oleg was down but not out. He looked at his watch and up to the towering figure of the Laughing Buddha. Eleven o'clock on the dot.

Cody watched him for another ten minutes, counting the times he checked his watch, seeing him shuffle from foot to foot, the way he anxiously looked at passing tourists. All the while Cody checked that Oleg was alone. 'Smile!' He detached himself from a bunch of kids and their teachers and pushed the camera into Oleg's face. Cody took a picture and spoke in fluent Russian. 'Comrade, welcome to Singapore – ice cream?'

'Oleg you don't look so bad with your clothes on!' Cody was in a playful, mischievous mood. 'But seriously we can make this as pleasant as possible or revert to the old ways. We sometimes use the tried and tested techniques, but delivered in a more modern way. I'm going to switch back to English, if that's okay.' Oleg's mind was in a whirl. 'Let's talk professional to professional. You know we have photos and a reel of Oscar nominated footage – and, before you say anything it is kept in a very safe place – and I'm not talking about the vault at the HSBC branch in Orchard

Road.' Cody had lowered his voice and talked very slowly at the mention of the HSBC bombing, crudely telegraphing his suspicion that somehow the Russians were involved. 'If we co-operate we can serve our masters and have a good reason to keep you alive and able to enjoy the odd night on the town – capiche?'

'I was expecting to be abducted not offered an ice cream.' Oleg's stress levels fell rapidly.

'Let's see if we can work something out – without getting heavy. I've got another envelope in my pocket and guess what? No film inside!' Cody beamed, cracking up at his own joke. 'Let's call it a small token to make up for the shock this morning.' Cody finally got to the point. 'In return for all this goodwill and understanding there's a price to pay - an exchange of values. We'd like you to be on our payroll as an information gatherer. The first piece of information we'd like is the names of the people responsible for the MacDonald building bombing – just that, easy. You have a week.'

The meeting was over.

SIX

9.30am Monday 15th March 1965. The Headquarters of the 6-6-6 Triad, Bukit Timah Hill, Singapore.

Freddie Burton waited to join Jonny Lau in his state of the art office somewhere off the Upper Thomson Road. The heavily fortified building was set in idyllic natural surroundings on Bukit Timah Hill. Palms, Frangipani, Rambutan and Durian trees provided a scenic and protective barrier from prying eyes. Freddie could never understand why the fruit of the durian tree tasted so sweet yet smelled so foul. Bukit Timah had the lush vegetation and wondrous plant and animal wildlife of a tropical forest. Thick moss covered rocks like a perfectly fitted carpet. Wild orchids and crimson bougainvillea nestled by ponds and clung to walls. Bats, pangolins and long-tailed macaque monkeys could be found above ground, while dragon fish swam languorously in sculptured ponds. The oriental kingfisher was a kaleidoscope of colour as it rocketed through the sky. All these beautiful creatures shared this blissful tropical retreat.

It was a strange juxtaposition; natural harmony inhabited by men who debased the rules of nature.

The fact that Freddie had been kept waiting did not faze him at all. He could hear voices behind the thick outer doors in a heated conversation. He chose to sharpen his senses with another favourite meditation technique. This technique served him well, helping to focus the mind and improve concentration. It worked like this. Freddie separated sounds into three distinct zones. Those close by, ones in the middle distance, and those further away. He concentrated on each sound zone in turn. Freddie found that with practice he could mentally shift from zone to zone, opening and closing sounds as he went.

It was as if his ears were highly-tuned radar discs sweeping the air for important signals. The practical benefit was that he could pick up the voices or sounds in any of these three zones and mask out any disturbance or disruption. This allowed him to listen to the voices of a man and a woman behind the heavy doors. He caught snatches of Mandarin but could not make complete sense of it. Freddie was certain he recognised the woman's voice but from where? Freddie heard an inner door slam shut.

The outer door remained closed for a moment longer - long enough for Jannah to make her exit unseen. Jonny Lau watched her go and remembered the first time they'd met. It was five years ago. Two young kids wanting a tourist trip on their first day in Singapore. They'd waved down his rickshaw from all the hundreds of rickshaws. They'd started to get to know each other on that day. Today Jannah was the manager of The Dragon Club and pressing to become his deputy. A woman as second in command of a Triad was unheard of. There again, she had used her skills to bring an MI6 agent to his door...

Freddie was convinced it couldn't be Jannah. He'd left her in bed and come straight to this meeting. Anyway, what would she be doing here at the headquarters of a criminal gang? No, not possible, he'd concentrate on the meeting and put the idea out of his mind. It was a female voice that reminded him of Jannah because he was thinking of her, simple as that.

The first time Jannah and Freddie met, she was waiting tables. Her eyes and her smile directed only on him, slicing through his defences, sending pulses surging like rippling tentacles through his body. She came over to him. Freddie was about to speak as the words were choked off by her soft lips pressing on his. The tip of her tongue darted inside his mouth; an act of uninhibited penetration. It was the final hook that reeled him in. In front of everyone, without a care, she flung her head back joyfully laughing amid wild applause for her erotic performance.

Freddie's daydream evaporated.

'Mr Burton, Mr Yip Chung Lau is ready to see you now, he's sorry to keep you waiting.' Jonny Lau's PA, dressed in a western business suit, beckoned him to follow. She took him through an interconnecting steel door to his office and inner sanctum. The two influences, one of commerce, the other of spirituality, blended in comfortable harmony. Jonny's circular desk of polished teak held accounting ledgers and files, a red phone and a black one: black for legal business, red for criminality. The mandatory abacus, worn and shiny from constant use, was momentarily resting from tallying overnight takings.

An enormous window of bullet-proof glass opened onto the garden and revealed the criss-crossing sentries patrolling below. The walls were hung with 18 pictures of Shaolin martial art routines in delicate yet vivid brushwork. In the corner was a shrine draped in vibrant deep orange silk, the colour of Buddhist robes. Candle flames in the shrine flickered on nothingness. In the centre, in the place of honour, there was nothing, nothing but an empty wooden plinth waiting for something to be placed on it.

Jonny wore the gang colours of a black cheongsam jacket with a dragon motif embroidered on the left breast, lightweight black trousers and leather sandals. His handshake was firm without flexing the power of his forearm, hinting at hidden strength. It was the most subtle of welcomes that telegraphed an unmistakable message to Freddie that he was in the presence of a man to be feared and respected. He stood just less than two metres tall, his head shaved; his lined face reflected a life well lived and was a movable mask of moods. One moment open and smiling: the next cold as stone. His eyes missed nothing. For Freddie he adopted the friendly mask.

'I read your letter with great interest. In these troubled times I think we share some common ground.' Jonny's voice ended with a question mark.

'I believe so.' Freddie started to outline his plan. 'We have a mutual enemy, one that's causing damage to your business, and our country. I have respect for you and the way you fought in the Japanese occupation, none of us want to go through that again.' Jonny had anticipated what Freddie would say. He'd guessed half of it. The other half got him really excited.

'We need a two pronged attack.' Freddie continued warming to the task. 'First, we need to go against the saboteurs operating on the island. We need to create a united force comprising 6-6-6 and the other street gangs to put an end to these bombings. Can you host a meeting with the other gang leaders? If they agree to join the fight, our side of the bargain is to put pressure on the Police to turn a blind eye on your operations for a time. It would be a kind of amnesty.'

Jonny recalled his street map of gangland Singapore concept. Jonny particularly liked the idea of an amnesty to recoup his recent losses.

Freddie revealed the next part of his plan. 'The second point of attack is to take the battle to the Indonesians. Gangland Singapore will fight back.' Freddie had a wicked gleam in his eyes.

'This will be a secret covert operation. We will attack the insurgent base on Bintan Island and level it to the ground. The force will comprise your finest 6-6-6 fighters and the cream of gangland enforcers. Our special operations personnel will command the assault. The force will be a lethal combination of underworld and military black-ops expertise. The force will be called The Katong Irregulars, after the recent attack on the Katong Grange Hotel.'

Freddie's words struck home. Jonny relived the long and painful seconds of Kim's last goodbye and grasped the momentous significance of what lay ahead. This was a golden opportunity in every sense. Here was a way to strengthen his personal position, to strike a deal with the authorities, and most importantly, to regain an item beyond price. Jonny turned to the empty plinth making an almost imperceptible, respectful, inflection of his head. He then extended his hand in agreement. The handshake was one of mutual respect.

All Freddie had to do was explain his plan to the British Army High Command, get the CIA to buy into it, gain approval from the Singapore Defence Force and clear it with the Royal Navy and Air Force. Piece of cake. He decided to start with Cody. That would need some secret messages delivered through his schoolboy network.

***

Cody was sitting by the sea wall at the Singapore Swimming Club. He'd had a fine time using the one, three and five metre diving boards, balancing on the balls of his feet, springing upwards, with his ankles together to pierce the water with hardly a ripple. This was followed by a few lengths of the pool trying to get his breathing right, drying off, applying the suntan cream and feeling the sun on his face. He wasn't missing Vietnam one little bit. He was in a particularly upbeat mood.

Two names were written on a folded piece of paper inside his wallet. Harun Said and Osman Ali, members of the Indonesian Marine Corps, had been identified as the Macdonald House bombers. Oleg had delivered within the week. In exchange, some photo negatives were sent from Cody along with a promise of more to follow.

Cody's good mood was tinged with the worry that it had been too easy. Perhaps he should be more wary of Oleg and not make the mistake of taking him for granted. He could be hatching a devious plot to snare his own prize for the KGB with Cody as the target. It would be easy to arrange a killing in a back alley or unexpected daylight abduction. Cody's ability to anticipate danger had never let him down. Something was telling him not to relax, especially while his body was soaking up the heat of the sun. He should never forget he was a soldier in a cold war.

Cody had no need to worry. Oleg was taking the long view. If he was to become a double agent he had a few tricks up his sleeve and was a master of the double-cross. He would pick the time and place for any action. In the short term, Oleg knew that Cody would not be working alone and the incriminating evidence would be tucked away in a secure hiding place. This could be anywhere, in the Far East or even the United States, to be used against him if anything happened to a CIA operative. Since arriving in Singapore Oleg's intelligence reports showed the strength of the Allied Forces. He knew the Indonesians with their outmoded Soviet weaponry would be no match for the American, British and Australian firepower.

In a way, his Bugis Street mistake might prove his salvation, his escape strategy. He was dealing directly with the Americans. If he was useful to them, they could be useful to him. No, he would bide his time and see how things developed.

Oleg loved the irony of glorious wickedness being a potential passport to a new life.

As it happened, Chris was also at the Singapore Swimming Club. Freddie's message for Cody wrapped in his towel. He wanted to make sure that Freddie's description fitted the man by the sea wall before he made contact. In the meantime, Chris was pacing the steps from his position to the end of the springboard. The movement would be one step forward leading with his left foot, then on the second step he would reach the end of the board. With his two feet together he'd spring into the air to make his dive. His instructor watched from the side of the pool to see whether his pupil was good enough to compete for his Bronze diving certificate.

After the drama of their first night in Singapore, the Blake family had settled into a measured routine at the Katong Grange Hotel. As school finished at three o'clock, Chris and Debbie would be back at the swimming club for a late afternoon session. They signed for drinks and plates of chips, smothered in Heinz Tomato Ketchup, at the end of their swimming lessons. Cody's identity was confirmed when a waiter walked round the pool holding a blackboard with a name written in chalk. The board held a small bell that he occasionally pinged as he walked. 'Telephone call for Mr Jackson: Call for Mr Jackson.' Chris completed his dive, legs too wide, over-rotated and ended with a dreadful splash.

When Cody returned to his table from taking the phone call, Freddie's envelope had magically appeared. Chris peered through his towel as he dried his hair to see that the message had been securely delivered and went to change. Cody read the message:

'Fried Oysters, Chilli Crab, Beef Rendang, Nasi Goreng - Meet me at Bedok Corner tonight at nine. Exciting Times! Food on Me. Freddie.'

Freddie sat looking out to sea as the waves nudged the land. He was reflecting on what was happening and what was about to happen. He was on his own, but he was not alone; a colourful circus of activity buzzed around him. The food stalls thronged with controlled chaos, the vibrant bustle of stallholders were calling out, wanting to attract as many stomachs to their delicious food as possible. The cooks moved at a frenzied pace, burning oil flaring in flames as the scorching woks were set to work.

Freddie felt totally at home inside this riotous bedlam. Offshore the pile-drivers had been at work sinking metal pillars into the sand. The first stage of reclaiming land from the sea was underway. Soon Bedok Corner would be inland and no longer at the seafront. Freddie understood the need for more land for housing. His fear was that Singapore would sell its soul in the process, and all that he loved would be lost in the drive for relentless progress.

'Penny for your thoughts?' Cody appeared beside him.

'Kelongs.' Freddie replied.

'What are Kelongs?' Cody wondered if the word was an insult.

'The Kelongs that are not here anymore,' Freddie replied enigmatically.

'C'mon brother, shine a light.' Freddie understood Cody's request for information and spoke.

'A Kelong is the Malay word for an offshore fishing trap. It's an ingenious idea. Bamboo or plain wooden stakes are driven into the sand side by side to create an underwater fence, one that encourages fish to swim along it. The stakes are expertly angled to take account of the prevailing winds and tides. At the end of the barrier, fishermen build a bamboo hut propped up on longer stakes. The hut has floor boards and a living area where they rest and eat. In the middle of the floor is an open space where a bright lantern hangs over the water. A net is lowered into the sea. The lantern attracts the fish. The fish swim happily along the wooden fence and straight into the net. It is such a brilliant concept, a great design and unfailing functionality.'

'So what's the problem?' Cody was enjoying talking about fish as a change from undercover work.

'They've been destroyed to make way for the reclamation. The locals have been moved to the Upper Changi Road estate and away from Bedok Corner.' Freddie decided to change the subject. 'So what's it to be? Fried oysters, cuttlefish, Hokkien Mee fried noodles?' An hour of beer and banter later, Cody couldn't stand the suspense any longer he had to know what Freddie meant by his message.

'Exciting times, exciting news – give, what's occurring?'

Freddie thought he would slowly build up to revealing the plan he'd outlined to Jonny Lau to assess Cody's reaction. 'When we first met you said – and I quote – "Covert is good". Well, I've devised an operation. The risks are great but so are the rewards.' Cody telegraphed his interest by locking his eyes on Freddie and felt his pulse quicken. This was the kind of intrigue he lived for.

'Go on.'

'When the Japanese invaded Singapore in 1942, the captured Allied prisoners were sent to Burma to build railways, to Changi Gaol, or to certain death in prisoner of war camps. During the subsequent occupation of the island, criminal gangs in Singapore carried out guerrilla attacks against the Japs. They knew they would suffer reprisals but they needed to protect themselves, their businesses, and fellow Singaporeans.'

'And your point?' Cody wanted to rush ahead to the punch line.

Freddie needed to set the scene so Cody could fully grasp the full drama of the idea.

'The 6-6-6 Triad was a leader in the fight.'

'Yes! – And?' Cody's fingers were tapping impatiently, his shoulders flexing in anticipation.

'We're going back to 1942. Jonny Lau, the leader of the 6-6-6 gang is calling all the other gangs together to take the war to the Indonesians. And we're going to run it!'

Cody's smile was the sun coming out.

'There's just one thing.' Freddie gave Cody the time to take a mouthful of Tiger beer.

'I've told Jonny that we've got the backing of the British and the Singapore authorities. I've told Jonny that the gangs will win a pardon. The thing is, we haven't got any support and they won't get a pardon.' Freddie waited.

'Well, we'll just have to be a little creative. I guess what they don't know can't hurt them; the top brass that is. Criminals are criminals after all. No one's going to lose sleep if a few bad boys don't come home.'

Freddie reached for his Tiger. Two bottles clinked in unison to seal the pact.

SEVEN

Tuesday 13th April 1965. The Indonesian Marine Corps Naval Base, Batam Island.

The melodic strains of a clarinet carried gently on the sultry night air. The clinging heat and humidity giving each note incredible depth and fullness as the sound snaked invisibly between the beachfront palms and across the white sand in a lilting lullaby.

Captain Arto Hakim was playing and thinking, thinking and playing. His crew were used to it. They lay in their bunks ashore knowing their skipper had turned his night into day and was working through until dawn solving problems. Working at night avoided interruptions and allowed him to think deeply without being disturbed by petty commands from Headquarters or ringing phones. After returning from the meeting with Oleg Rozanov, Arto was expected to formulate a plan of action against the Allies. This meant putting his head into the lion's mouth.

Arto was alone in the operations room, standing before a wall covered with British Admiralty Charts. The focus of his attention was Admiralty Chart 4044, the Eastern Part of the Johor Straits, the stretch that was heavily patrolled by minesweepers protected by air bases at Tengah, Seletar and Changi. The question was how could Arto do his duty without putting lives needlessly at risk? Any attack would be suicidal.

Arto was told to prepare a plan to block the entrance to the Johor Straits. He'd assembled wooden models of submarines, minefields and motor torpedo boats. Plastic soldiers were spread on a map like action-man figures. While his military brain was considering a multitude of options, the other side of his brain was restless. He'd resisted pressure to join the communist party. He also knew that tensions were rising within the military between factions that favoured the PKI and those who had more nationalist leanings and were anti-communist. Arto had a feeling that matters in the Indonesian Army would soon come to a head. If the nationalists gained power, the confrontation fighting would be ended. He had a dread of leading his men into action just as peace was declared. He sometimes thought of those soldiers in the First World War, killed moments before the clock struck eleven, on the eleventh day of the eleventh month.

He put down his clarinet, wiped the mouthpiece, checked the reed and lay the much loved instrument into its case. He slid his scratched record of Mozart's Clarinet Concerto out of its battered brown sleeve and placed it on the turntable. At two in the morning he decided on his strategy: do nothing, play for time. Sun Tzu's book, The Art of War, was a prized possession; its well-thumbed pages lay on his desk. A passage leapt from the page. 'All warfare is based on deception: hence, when able to attack, we must seem unable; when using our forces, we must seem inactive; when we are near, we must make the enemy believe we are far away; when far away, we must make him believe we are near.'

'Deception.'

Arto spoke the word out loud. He stopped the record player, turned off the light and went to bed with a crafty smile on his face.

***

Joe's in Changi Village was the favourite meeting and messaging point. Chris was about to sink his teeth into a giant cheese roti bread roll, when Joe himself handed him a message from Freddie. His mates were bunched round a worn wooden table and sat on three-legged stools. It was Tuesday evening and the whole village was given over to rows of stalls selling everything under the sun in the Amah's market.

For the kids, the most important was the music stall that sold all the latest chart releases from the UK and America. Kobz had left to check out the new arrivals and was flicking through the box of 45 rpm singles that included The Temptations with 'My Girl', Tom Jones with 'It's Not Unusual', The Beatles with 'Eight Days a Week' and The Stones with 'The Last Time'. Kobz spun the record over to see the B-side of Playing with Fire. He reached into his jeans for the few dollars he possessed.

Chris studied the handwritten envelope that simply had his initials CB on the outside and this note on the inside.

'Chris – Fancy a Sail? I need an experienced crew member to help me bring Galadriel round to the yacht club from Singapore harbour where she's had an overhaul. It will take just a few hours on Saturday. I'll have a couple of friends on-board for the trip.

See you here at Joe's 10am Saturday. I'll make it worth your while. Bring a girlfriend if you want. Cheers Freddie.'

Chris was reading contentedly until he got to BRING A GIRLFRIEND. The invitation leapt off the page and grabbed him by the throat. Chris went from calm to panic with an explosion of hooters and sirens going off in his brain, a girl, a girlfriend, a friend who's a girl! How would he get a girlfriend in three days? Seeing his startled reaction, all eyes gripped him.

'Got it – Downtown by Petula Clark!' Kobz pounced on a stool and broke the spell.

Ridicule had a new target. 'Eewweh' said Dave Wickett.

Nick Shilling put his fingers in his mouth. 'Pass the bucket, I need to vomit.'

'As if!' Kobz joked. 'The Kinks -'Tired of Waiting for You'!'

'Wanker!' Dave Tommo was a man of few words.

Chris used this timely diversion to think of something to say, something to sound convincing without giving too much away. He needed to protect his secret relationship with Freddie. 'Oh, just been asked to crew for somebody at the yacht club on Saturday – no drama.'

Cheryl Williams lost interest completely. Chris Blake was not interesting anyway. Kobz changed the subject. 'Did you hear Dave Gamble has been suspended for throwing a snake in the girl's toilets?'

***

Fast forward four days. Saturday morning: 9.45am.

T-shirt, swimmies, towel, a cool bag with sandwiches, drinks and suntan cream, times two. Chris and Libby Stewart waited for Freddie to arrive at Joe's. They were both nervous but excited at the same time. Chris finally plucked up courage to ask Libby at school. Expecting a certain rebuff, he'd already turned away when she said 'Yes'.

Libby's blonde hair was tied back, her blue eyes darting up and down the road wondering what she'd let herself in for. She reasoned it would only be for a few hours and lovely to be out on a real sailing yacht. What could go wrong? Chris was painfully shy but she liked him because he was just that. He was nice, she didn't use the word 'sweet' as this was the kiss of death to boys, it meant girls didn't fancy them.

A Mercedes taxi drew up. Freddie gave Libby a warm hug of welcome and winked his approval to Chris. He explained. 'My two friends will be waiting at the boatyard for us. Galadriel's ready to go, so let's have some fun and create some memories.'

It was awkward. The first time Cody had seen Jannah at The Dragon Club he'd been blown away. Jannah was a fantasy on two legs. Here she was in the flesh, looking like a star, wearing the most fashionable wayfarer sunglasses and dressed as if she was going to a premiere, rather than spending a day out sailing. He should have made the connection between her and Freddie. When realisation finally dawned that they were a couple, it only increased his respect for Freddie. Jannah recognised and greeted Cody with an effusive smile and kisses on each cheek in the continental style. Their small talk was interrupted by the Mercedes arriving.

'Singapore Swimming Club, that's where I've seen you before.' Cody was all smiles with Chris. 'You were the mystery messenger!' Cody realised here was yet another element to Freddie Burton's web of contacts. Chris introduced Libby. 'Enchanté, mademoiselle.' Cody took Libby's hand and kissed it. Libby glowed with all the attention and loved mixing with such glamorous people. By knowing these people, perhaps Chris was not as dull as she first thought.

Galadriel, with her gleaming, sleek white hull, shiny brass fittings and teak decks, looked wonderful. Freddie and Chris stowed the gear and rigged the new set of sails recently arrived from Hood Sails in Lymington England. Freddie signed off the worksheet with the yacht yard and started the Volvo Penta engine to charge the batteries. Finally, he got ready to cast off. Freddie showed everyone where the life jackets and the Avon rubber dinghy were kept. Chris added the final touches of raising the Changi Yacht Club triangular cruising burgee flag at the top of the mast, slid the red ensign into the stern post, and tied thin strips of material as wind indicators to the wire side stays that supported the mast. They were ready for a short coastal trip.

Freddie took the helm. The fore and aft lines were cleared and rubber fenders taken inboard. The engine increased revs and Galadriel glided serenely into the crowded waters of Singapore harbour. Freddie beamed with pride and rung the ship's bell twice with everyone clapping. Cody announced Pimms o'clock and cheers rang out – Libby and Chris having an extra dilution of lemonade with theirs.

As soon as Galadriel had gained a little sea room to manoeuvre Freddie turned the bow into the wind.

This was the signal for Chris to go forward to raise the jib, the triangular sail in front of the mainsail. Freddie eased off the wind with the jib billowing and catching the breeze. The mainsail was slowly raised and Galadriel heeled slightly as the wind caught and filled the sail. Freddie cut the engine. The sound of the diesel motor was replaced by the almost silent rippling water and fine sea spray, the warm breeze blowing through the sails and the sweet music of wind plucking the metal support stays of the mast like a divine stringed instrument.

Galadriel was now fully under-sail and glorying in her element. Jannah hugged Libby, Cody toasted Freddie and Chris took the helm, giving him the chance to negotiate the many anchored merchantmen, giant tankers, Chinese junks and sampans with the preposterous confidence of youth. He helmed the 28 foot cruiser with a lightness of touch as if it was his Fireball racing dinghy.

Then the wind quietened and dropped away, not a whisper. Galadriel had sailed past the Katong Grange Hotel and was now becalmed off Bedok corner. They were within another hour's sailing before entering the Johor Strait and back safely to the yacht club. They were all in a happy and relaxed state of mind. Sandwiches were consumed and more Pimm's drunk. Libby applied the suntan cream. Chris drank coke as he was still at the helm.

An hour passed.

No sign of a breeze, not a single zephyr. Galadriel could feel that the underwater currents weren't resting. The flow was quickening as the tide changed, taking her almost discernibly further and further away from the shipping lanes. Freddie, Jannah and Cody were blissfully unaware of what was happening. Maybe it was because they thought they could rely on the ever reliable Volvo Penta. You could write the next line.

It didn't start.

The battery was faulty. The yard had put it on charge but not for long enough and they did not detect the seeping loss of power from ruptured battery cells. The charge was enough to kick start the engine in the dock but as Galadriel was so quickly under sail the battery did not gain enough kick to turn the engine over. The yacht had no short wave or VHF radio. As night fell they were pushed out of sight of land. There was a little charge to power the navigation lights, including the white light at the top of the mast. They were wishing they'd brought some warm clothing.

The vast South China Sea or the enemy islands of Indonesia would be their next stop.

On land, the alarm had been raised by the sailing officer at the yacht club. Freddie had logged their trip and an estimated time of arrival of hours before. Galadriel was long overdue and, with no reported sightings, 205 Squadron was alerted. An RAF Shackleton Marine Search and Rescue aircraft was scrambled. The crew plotted a search grid square calculating the speed of drift and currents from the south eastern coast of Singapore. The radar and visual search commenced.

On board, a vain attempt had been made to inflate the Avon rubber dinghy and tow Galadriel to minimise the inexorable drift. The weight of the boat made the effort totally useless. It was now nine at night. Fatigue set in. Freddie set up a watch system to allow some to rest while others trained the binoculars on a flat sea and black night hoping to find some sign of life. The navigation and cabin lights were turned on and off in fifteen minute intervals to save power, plunging Galadriel into darkness. There was no moonlight to catch the white of the sails.

The slumbering yacht was suddenly jolted sideways. Boarding lines were thrown and camouflaged marines stormed the boat. The soldier's faces were hidden under jungle hats and smeared with stripes of black and green.

'Ladies and gentlemen, the Singapore Defence Force is here to offer assistance.' Michael Yeo, the gunboat skipper, gave the order to attach a towline.

One of the soldiers stayed in the shadows of the gunboat. He watched as the day-trippers hugged and kissed and repeated their thanks over and over again. The soldier recognised Freddie and saw him grasp his girlfriend tightly and witnessed their emotional embrace.

Billy Chang immediately recognised Jannah. He remembered her with crystal clarity.

EIGHT

Monday 26th April 1965, 6-6-6 Headquarters. A plan unfolds.

Lee Jaya's heart rate was pumping at 190 beats per minute. His body was reaching the limits of exertion as he finished the morning's martial arts training session. Lee led a team of enforcers in a gruelling programme based on the routines of the Shaolin warrior monks. These handpicked men and women formed the squad who would take the honour of the 6-6-6 Triad into battle. The squad of two women and four men had passed the initiation and over the last month had attended morning and evening sessions to sharpen their skills that included the Iron Body technique that mentally directed energy to different parts of the body to withstand and channel pain inflicted during merciless rounds of training.

The candidates achieved incredible feats of fitness of scaling walls and balancing on the tops of poles to improve balance and dexterity as well as pressure point and nerve manipulation. They were expert in the use of Wushu combat weaponry. of throwing knives, deadly throwing discs in the shape of stars that zipped through the air silently to their targets and traditional swords tempered to a razor's edge. All this added to their armed skills with pistols, machineguns and explosives. The team were now going through a series of cooling down exercises before inspection by Jonny Lau.

Lee was in agony. An agony that had nothing to do with physical pain: but everything to do with a broken heart.

Behind the stone-faced inscrutability hid a passionate man. He had always been Jannah's protector and lover. In the early days, both Lee and Jannah shared the communist ideal, fighting hard and losing themselves in uninhibited, life-affirming sex after guerrilla raids, escaping death and embracing the life-force until they were totally spent.

Lee accepted that Jannah used her beauty as an impersonal deadly weapon. She became a Praying Mantis, the female who'd seduce before killing the male of the species. They both accepted this as a dispassionate weapon in her armoury; dealing the sweetness of sex before striking a fatal blow. The same alluring trap she had sprung on Rifleman Alan Jenkins on Tioman Island all those years ago. The enticing snare that ended his life.

***

Singapore had changed all that. Jannah had been slipping slowly away from him for over a year. He was always her second in command. Now, he was a poor second to pretty much everyone. Her rise within the 6-6-6 Triad, becoming manager and controller of The Dragon Club, had fractured their relationship. She had grown. He was yesterday. To top it all, her Praying Mantis role no longer applied to Freddie

Burton. Freddie was supposed to be the enemy, an agent of the British MI6, now lines were confusingly blurred. Lee was not sure of anything anymore.

Jonny Lau strode onto the balcony overlooking the training ground. The squad saluted by right fists striking left breasts. Jonny raised both arms high with two clenched fists in response.

'My fighters - you are agents of death and bringers of honour to the 6-6-6.' Jonny made eye contact with every member of the squad. 'You are now ready to undertake a special mission. Shortly, you will join an elite group, the cream of Singapore's street gangs. Together, we will attack and destroy the Indonesian base that sends saboteurs to kill our countrymen. We are going to strike back!' The squad emitted a devastating roar of approval, their voices creating a single wall of sound.

Ten silent seconds passed before he spoke again. 'This raid is a sacred mission for the 6-6-6, for too long our shrine of Guan Yu has remained empty. Candles have burned day and night waiting for his return. Your divine task is to bring back the golden statue, stolen by Indonesian pirates. It's your destiny to bring Guan Yu home!'

The squad erupted, chanting the name of Guan Yu over and over again. Jonny stepped back into the darkness of his office. He'd unleashed the dragons of war.

The enormity of what had just happened was a body blow to Lee. He faced a dilemma like never before. Up until that moment he'd controlled his duplicity with professional ease. He could maintain his links with the Indonesian insurgents in Singapore. He could manage his intelligence gathering relationship with Oleg and the Russians. He could trust Jannah not to compromise his communist sympathies. It had been a hard road to gain the trust of Jonny Lau and the rank and file of 6-6-6 enforcers.

What should he do now?

By joining the mission to attack the Indonesian base, Lee would be expected to leak information both to Oleg and his saboteur connections. If he did, then the mission would fail as his squad of enforcers walked into a hail of bullets. If he turned against the Indonesians he was committing suicide. If he turned against Jonny Lau he would lose Jannah forever. Lee could see no way out. A dead end was the only certainty.

***

Jonny knelt at the shrine. His mind flowed back through the years. He imagined the Emperor of the Ming dynasty in the sixteenth century calling upon the fighting skills of Buddhist monks to help protect against the Japanese pirates who ravaged the coast of China. The Shaolin monks were among the most feared and effective fighters. The golden statute of Guan Yu was taken by the Japanese pirates as contraband and found its way from China down to the Malacca Straits, a pirate haven for centuries.

The Malacca Straits are the maritime crossroads to the Far East linking the Indian Ocean via the Andaman Sea through the Singapore Straits, South China Sea and onward to the Pacific Ocean. Chinese porcelain, silks, peppercorns and spices were common cargoes and prime targets for Malacca Pirates in the Middle Ages, as well as crews of sailing ships sold as slaves or their passengers ransomed. There is a natural bottleneck known as the Phillips Channel. At this point, the Straits are less than three kilometres wide and surrounded by thousands of tiny islands offering secret hiding places among tangled mangrove swamps, inlets and dangerous reefs. Pirates, who knew every inch of the ground, attacked shipping then disappeared like phantoms into the surrounding countryside.

Jonny could chart the beginnings of the 6-6-6 to the arrival of Chinese labourers in the Nineteenth Century. On the 29th January 1819, Sir Stamford Raffles arrived in Singapore. At the time, the island was functioning as a poorly developed Portuguese trading post. Raffles set about establishing a base for the British East India Company. He saw the strategic and commercial potential and proceeded to build settlements that needed cheap Chinese Coolie labour to fuel the growth. At first, members of secret societies played a significant community role in looking after new arrivals, finding them shelter and looking after their families.

More Coolies meant more customers for gambling, opium, whores and protection; the staple diet of street gangs that inevitably led to turf wars and power struggles within the gangs. A pattern to be repeated and repeated to the present day.

Jonny's spies had got wind of a pirate settlement on the island of Bintan and the statue of Guan Yu was their prized possession. He would use the operation against the Indonesians as cover to achieve their real reason for joining the mission. It was time to reclaim history.

***

'We've got our taxi driver.' Freddie ticked a page on his notepad.

'Qué? Taxi driver? Qué es eso?' For some reason Cody was so confounded he started speaking Spanish. His linguistic talents went beyond Russian.

'Lieutenant Michael Yeo of the Singapore Defence Force, the commander of the launch that rescued us on Galadriel. He's agreed to run a little extra pleasure voyage to the lovely Indonesian holiday island of Bintan – as a piece of extra-curricular cruising. He knows the coastline and will be there under cover of the night to drop us and wait to bring us out.' Freddie answered.

'Aah I get you. You Brits have this weird sense of humour. I love the idea of taking a cab to a battle - and asking them to wait and return!'

'Look Cody, the more I put things together on this mission the more they fall apart. I promised training under our supervision – couldn't get clearance. I promised SAS involvement – not happening, the idea is too irregular even for the SAS. I promised arms and ammunition – can't get it. I promised an amnesty – no chance. It looks as though we'll have to go so covert that no-one knows this mission exists, except us, and all we'll get is a promise to turn a blind eye on the night of the raid.'

'Yeah, but look on the bright side – no interference. It's our party, isn't that what we live for?' Cody had a mischievous glint in his eye. 'Bring it on!'

'You're right. Let's prepare for the briefing tomorrow with our criminal comrades. One thing though. As you don't speak Mandarin and don't look Chinese, I think you should sit this out and meet me in Chinatown for a beer afterwards.'

'Makes sense – but I'm coming on the raid – I need to kick some ass – I haven't misbehaved for so long!' Cody was so up for it.

'Agreed. Here's to devilment with a rebel yell.' Freddie's nerve-ends were sparking with excitement.

The boys craved the intoxication of danger.

***

Sago Lane is known as the street of death.

Shophouses line both sides of Sago Lane, so called, because shops leading onto the street are turned into funeral parlours at ground level and above them the upper floors are the houses of death. Terminally ill, elderly poor and destitute lie in dark dormitories clustered together on narrow metal beds in the final hours of their lives. The upper windows offer little protection against the North-West Monsoon and now in April with temperatures soaring to over 30 degrees they struggle for breath in the heat.

As they reached their last moments they would hear noise filtering upwards. The sounds of mourners attending someone else's funeral. Burning incense creates clouds of pungent, acrid smoke, dirges played on string instruments and the wailing of distraught relatives drift can be heard. Some, on the verge of death, glimpse their coffins being carved from wood, waiting for their rigid corpses. If they're fortunate, and have a few dollars to spend, they may have paid for paper models of a lovely house, a car or other possessions that will surely follow them into the afterlife. Hell Money is burned to keep away vengeful ghosts and spirits.

As they lie awake at night, they'd hear the lively clatter from nearby restaurants or hawker stalls set up in the road. Cries of passion from brothels mingle with these earthly sounds. Life and death living side by side in one continuous circle.

It was a touch of genius. Jonny had decided on a funeral parlour as the meeting place of the Triads. Representatives of the street gangs gathered slowly, disguised as mourners. They wore the traditional hessian hooded cowls that completely covered their heads and fell like rug cloaks over their shoulders and backs. They kept their faces down and adopted a stooping gait as they mingled with other mourners and street sellers; some even used walking sticks to give the impression of being feeble and ancient.

Jonny chose to hold the meeting in broad daylight to add a measure of the unexpected to fool the Police and Security Forces. Imagine what would happen if the Police knew the most dangerous members of the Singapore underworld were meeting together under one roof. Jonny rose to his feet. He didn't have to speak to get the attention of the other eight most powerful gang bosses in Singapore, just standing up was enough.

'Thank you for coming; this will be a short but important meeting. History is repeating itself. The gangs joined forces to fight the Japanese. We need to join together again. These bombings by the Indonesian insurgents disrupt our business. Our livelihoods are threatened and our country is under attack. We have to fight back and not behave like frightened children.' Jonny Lau nodded to Freddie to take the stage. 'And we are not alone.'

Freddie stood in front of a map ironically covered with a white shroud. 'What I'm about to tell you is Top Secret. Pass on this information only to trusted members of your organisations.' Freddie had to hide his nervousness at being in the company of these criminals, people who were responsible for inflicting torture and dispensing death without a second's thought. Freddie removed the shroud to reveal Bintan, the largest of the Riau Islands and directly across the Singapore Straits.

'I'm here to brief you on Operation Macdonald, named after the recent Macdonald House bombing. Our target is the Indonesian guerrilla base on the island of Palau Bintan. The base is situated near the coastal town of Berakit in the north. Our objective is to raze it to the ground. We will not attack innocent civilians, women and children. Our strike force will need your most ferocious fighters. The force will land on the island from a Singapore Defence Force launch. A secret reconnaissance mission to gather intelligence and lay explosive charges will be undertaken by members of the SAS before the raid. The speed and surprise of our attack will be our greatest advantage.' Freddie drew breath and waited for a reaction.

Silence. No one spoke. It was as Freddie expected. These gangs know the importance of face. By attending the meeting the gang bosses had agreed by their presence alone to support the operation.

This would be a question of honour among peers. Dishonour from non-involvement would be a slight they would carry forever.

One by one they stood and formed a circle round Jonny and extended their right arms like spokes in a wheel, their bodies became a symbolic ring of steel. It was a solemn commitment. All inter-gang rivalry would be put on hold until the operation was over.

Freddie was right about maintaining face – but two-faced? He put aside worries about not telling the whole truth. Lying was a way of life to these men. He did wonder what scores would be settled between gangs when the bullets started to fly. Freddie decided it was not worth thinking about. What happens, happens.

NINE

27th April 1965. Post Triad Meeting, Chinatown.

Freddie was in a trance. He was sitting alone at a table with an untouched beer, staring into the middle distance. It was as if he was the centrepiece of a time lapse film, with masses of people surging and streaming in waves around him. Freddie was oblivious to everything. His mind was far away, out of body, inside a private reality. The enormity of what happened during the Sago Lane meeting, of the agreement to his plans, of the dangers that lay ahead, had crashed into his brain like a reckless, sensory avalanche.

Since childhood Freddie had been an observer, an outsider. Being Eurasian he straddled cultures and found himself exposed to the best and worst of each. Identity confusion was a constant companion. One moment, he wished to be a cricket-playing English school boy, the next, to be a Martial Arts black belt, accepted by the Chinese community. As a child, he didn't know who he was. As an adult, he appreciated the benefits of bridging cultures. He became a human chameleon, changing appearance and attitude to suit both. His performance at the Sago Lane meeting made him realise that after all these years he'd finally been accepted and trusted for his talent alone. It was a landmark day.

Freddie was so deeply immersed that he didn't react to the graunching noise of three metal chairs being moved, or the sound of three heavy bodies settling on wooden seats, nor the penetrating looks from three intense weather beaten and battle-scarred Chinese faces.

'Freddie, Freddie - are you in there?' Billy Chang's voice attempted to bridge the ethereal space between him and Freddie's consciousness. 'I'd like to introduce Alex Jung and George Shiu, my mates from Special Ops, and now working with me in the Singapore Defence Force. They were on the launch that rescued Galadriel.' The mention of Galadriel coaxed Freddie's mind to climb back to reality. Freddie's eyelids flickered and sprang open.

'Ha! Sorry was deep in thought, glad to meet you guys.' Freddie shook hands then reached for his beer. 'Guys - can I buy you a drink?'

'Our skipper, Michael Yeo, briefed us on the trip to Bintan Island and that you needed a reconnaissance mission.' Billy had switched to speaking Mandarin but kept his voice low as you never knew who would be listening. Speaking fluent English would immediately draw attention to the group. 'Alex and George wanted to meet you.' Fresh cold Tigers and a mixed plate of chicken and prawn satay were placed on the table and swiftly consumed, leaving only the bamboo sticks as tooth picks.

'I've known Alex and George since we were kids in Vancouver. Our families first came over from China in the 1880s to work construction on the Canadian Pacific railroad. Here we're in the deconstruction business!' Billy grinned at his own joke. 'We watch each other's backs, like the Chinese version of the three musketeers. Alex and George are experts in demolition, the kind of skills you need.'

This was music to Freddie's ears. 'Really glad to meet you guys. We need to pay a visit to a certain exotic beachfront location in preparation for a bigger trip to the seaside sometime soon. It'll be dangerous but essential.'

'We do danger.' Billy, Alex and George finished their beers and disappeared. Before their seats got cold, Cody appeared.

He arrived with a Qantas air hostess on each arm. 'Work, work, work, what's a poor boy to do?' Cody was at his mischievous best. He mouthed two letters 'o' and 'k' with a question mark in his eyes to ask how the Sago Lane meeting went. Freddie responded by mouthing back 'g-o-o-d'. That was all the business spoken that night. The girls needed to be entertained.

***

Oleg's network of spies had been keeping a close eye on Cody. The spies were briefed to watch and report his movements. His contacts were reporting that after the Macdonald House bombing, insurgent activity had been concentrated on the mainland away from Singapore. Oleg noticed a hardening of resolve against the confrontation. In Singapore, groups of vigilantes were being formed as an extra resource for the security services. Added to this, he'd not had any contact with Lee Jaya for some weeks. Perhaps this was the most ominous signal of all. Did it mean that the tide was turning, was it time to reconsider his tactics? Cody had not applied any great pressure on him personally. Occasionally a single photo would arrive. It was a pointed reminder of power over him. Enough to keep him underperforming on the intelligence front, enough to give him options if he decided to part the Iron Curtain and walk through it to the other side.

Oleg did not destroy the graphic blackmail pictures. He kept them all in a safe place and away from his KGB colleagues. He liked looking at them. They excited him. Not only that, he'd become a member of The Dragon Club. He would be assured of their code of silence and he could indulge his passions. Oleg reasoned that it was he who got drunk that night. It was him that was willingly led astray. It was him that loved every minute. Recently he'd been enjoying more than minutes at the champagne bar and many occasions enjoying the company of handsome young men and the Ladyboys of Bugis Street.

His hair was growing longer. He found himself singing 'Love Me Do' by those Beatles, with a Ukrainian accent. Oleg had even indulged himself with several dabs of the degenerate capitalist aftershave, Old Spice and discarded his rough cotton boxers for a new pair of American style Y-fronts. Oleg had become a double agent in the purest sense. He was one person for his bosses and one for himself. Liberation was a dizzying drug. He still remained KGB but with a capitalist twist. As long as he could control the two identities, he would owe Cody a big favour.

Jannah was assessing her options too. She'd come a long way from dicing with death in the jungle. The operational skills developed under duress fighting with the Malayan Communist Party, the experience of being a unit commander and taking command was not dramatically different from knowing how to motivate, manage and manipulate people at The Dragon Club and within the 6-6-6. Plus, there were fewer bullets aimed in her direction. The Singapore effect was having a strong positive influence. By being part of the underworld she had gained status that demanded respect. A respect that had gone beyond her physical attributes, it was recognition of her intelligence and the influence she possessed with Jonny Lau. Jonny valued the contribution she made to the smooth running of the club and sought her counsel on 6-6-6 issues too.

Privately, Jannah was more selective in the use of her sexuality. It was now applied when either the stakes or the rewards were high. She still valued Lee's love and loyalty, the difference was that her confidence had no limits, she believed she could achieve whatever she set her mind to. In Freddie, she saw someone who as well as having the looks of a film star, had intelligence, sensitivity and the same aptitude and love for scheming she had. It was a potent combination, especially as they both knew they were playing a game, a game with added spice. They knew their relationship was a cat and mouse affair, never quite knowing who was the cat and who was the mouse. When together, intellectually and physically, they made the perfectly imperfect couple.

☆ ☆ ☆

It's a fact that adolescent schoolboys have only one brain cell each. This was particularly true for Kobz and Chris except that on this day by Changi Creek, the intelligence level was so low they shared one lonely brain cell between them.

They'd discovered Chinese fireworks. They became an all-consuming passion that rendered them practically brain dead. These were not everyday firecrackers that added machine-gunning, rat-a-tat, sparky, annoying bangs during Lion dancing or street festivals, but the ones that were a credit to the ancient Chinese tradition of fireworks that set the world alight with flashes, crashes and enormous, ear-splitting bangs.

These creations are a potent threat to the survival of the human race, or in this case, the foolish race of small boys. Their arsenal included Thunderboxes. These were heavy grade bangers in the form of round pellets that exploded against a hard surface, or as the boys quickly discovered, were a wicked weapon when shot from a catapult.

If you cut through the row of shops and stalls at the far end of Changi Village by the bus terminal, there's a mud path that wiggles its way past shanty huts and kampong houses down to the creek. A narrow footbridge spans the water to Changi Beach on the far side. The creek is jammed with launches, sampans and small fishing boats. At the weekend, kids would meet at Joe's then cram on the launches for island trips of swimming, diving and high jinks on the island of Palau Ubin.

The footbridge over the creek had a gentle raised curve at its centre. This became the duelling ground for Double Voice fireworks. One antagonist would stand on the north and one on the south side of the bridge. Double Voices were so called because they fired two separate explosive charges. Each contestant would place a Double Voice on top of the bridge wall and aim it at the other duellist. The blue touch paper would be lit and the duel would commence. A rippling spark and one piece of firework wadding would shoot out in an attempt to strike the opponent. After a heartbeat pause, the second shot of gunpowder would fire the second piece of wadding. As the wadding flew through the air the boys would duck and weave to avoid being hit.

It was only a short time before Chris noticed that the tubes of the Double Voices remained intact after both wads had been fired. The Double Voices would be picked up and aimed like the barrels of a gun. 'Aahah!' thought Chris. 'Here's a way to make the game even more exciting, just like cowboys, the black hats against the white hats facing each other in the heat of the noon-day sun.'

And so the next round of the hand-held conflict began. As it was Chris's idea, he took the first shot. He gripped the Double Voice between the thumb and index finger of his right hand. Odd really, because he was left handed, and lit the fuse. Bang went the first wad that flew straight and true but missed the astonished Kobz by a mile. A moment later, Chris felt the firework pulse in his hand, before emitting the second explosive wad. Success! The idea worked wonderfully, although more practice was needed to improve his aim.

Chris got ready for a second shot. Kobz was bobbing about like a manic goal-keeper, dodging left and right, ready to dive into the undergrowth to avoid any incoming artillery. Chris lit the fuse. He aimed, holding the firework away from his body and waited. The ring of fire glowed orangey-red as it advanced along the flimsy touch paper to ignite the gunpowder. Chris watched in slow motion as the first sparks triggered the bang and zinging flight of the first wad.

There was no second wad. There was a hand-held explosion.

His body and brain worked in two separate compartments. His body, sensing the immediate searing heat and shock of the explosion rushed adrenalin to his mutilated hand. His brain, experiencing an infinitesimal delay as the shock waves struck, reacted with stunned surprise then started to register intense slicing pain as nerve ends shredded, skin blackened and burned, nails ripped off and blood pumped.

Kobz reached him while Chris was still motionless, looking down at his throbbing hand with a look of incomprehension and disbelief on his face. While the boys had been playing there had been no-one at the creek side. No-one to tell them off, no-one to stop what they were doing. And no-one came. Chris had not made a sound, no cry, no scream of agony. The shock was so complete he remained silent.

Crimson blood coursed down his forearm streaming from his mangled fingers. Kobz carefully lifted Chris's yellow T-shirt and taking Chris's elbow, guided his hand under the soft cotton to cover the wound. The blood spiralled outward in an almost perfect circle. Taking his good hand, Kobz pulled Chris off the bridge and back up the mud track. As they reached the village people saw them and ran away shouting in panic.

'HE'S BEEN SHOT! THE BOY'S BEEN SHOT! WE'RE UNDER ATTACK!' 'THE INDONESIANS HAVE LANDED!'

TEN

Thursday 29 April 1965. Far East Operations Centre, CIA Secure Office.

'So, let's get this straight.' Cody was standing before the desk of his CIA Station Chief. 'You're joining a clandestine raid on an Indonesian island, without the knowledge of the top military command. The force is made up of fighters from the criminal underworld. A Singapore Defence Force Launch will disembark this untrained and unruly rabble – a rabble without clear leadership I might add – wait while the raid is being executed and bring you back, all in one night. The target is a heavily guarded military base that trains the saboteurs who've been committing these attacks against the Singapore civilian population. Sounds like a rabble without a cause. Is James Dean coming too? Is it being filmed for Hollywood? I guess Natalie Wood has been invited along for the boat trip and cocktails?' The station chief was just getting warmed-up, squeezing the acid juice of sarcasm from each bitter remark.

'That's pretty much it.' Cody counted to ten and tried to gauge the response before saying any more.

'This is not black ops, it's a black comedy. Who thought up this madness?' Cody explained the link with MI6, the business protection ethic of the Chinese underworld, of their pride and need to maintain face with other gangs and the loss of respect if they did nothing to stop these insurgents.

Twenty minutes later. 'Okay I get that. It does have a kind of Shakespearean tragedy ring about it. And I guess the loss of a few criminals would be a good thing, and the potential gains could make Langley smile on this piece of undiluted crap. Good thinking Cody Jackson, yeah, you've got the green light down the runway. Don't get captured – you hear me – we don't want any American involvement exposed!'

***

'A word in your ear.' Freddie was talking to Wing Commander Gareth Hughes, officer commanding 205 Squadron Shackletons, RAF Changi. Freddie chose to use that quaint form of language loved by British boarding school boys, intended to confuse a dastardly enemy, but was totally ridiculous. 'May the fifteenth, the night of the full moon, there's a special ops outing being arranged on the island of Bintan. Strictly invites only, old chap. The defence force is taking a small group of revellers to a bit of a do in one of their launches. The party starts at 0200 hours with carriages at dawn.'

Gareth began laughing as Freddie finished his terrible impersonation of an upper class idiot. 'I would take it as a personal favour if your airborne radar would mistake our movements for metal oil drums, or shoals of fish or anything but the truth?' Freddie had already given the squadron a case of the best champagne for spotting Galadriel and assisting in her safe return to Changi Yacht Club a couple of weeks earlier. As Singapore had controlled the airspace around the Riau Islands since 1946, Freddie was confident that there wouldn't be any problems from the air during the raid. He wanted to avoid any friendly fire incidents. At the same time, Freddie liked the idea of an airborne babysitter keeping a watchful eye over them.

'Mumm's the word.' Gareth displayed his knowledge of Champagne brands, a sense of humour and understanding of the request, all in the same instant. Freddie would owe him another case.

Freddie's round of preparations for the raid continued on-board HMS Fiskerton M1206, 8 Ton Coastal Minesweeper, Royal Naval Base Sembawang.

Captain Jeremy Crawford had listened to Freddie's request with interest. The Fiskerton was a member of the 6th Minesweeper Squadron and was on regular patrols off the Johor Straits to ensure the channels were clear of mines and intercept insurgent sampans.

Freddie and Jeremy were on first name terms. HMS Fiskerton had assisted covert landings in Borneo. Their shallow draught allowed the vessel to navigate upstream, placing elements from 42 Commando Royal Marines closer to the action.

Freddie thought it wise to recruit the navy as an escape Plan B, if the Singapore Defence Launch was forced to leave the action. It would be Fiskerton's brief to station the boat offshore to watch and wait. If the raid ran into difficulties, they would rendezvous off the Horsburgh lighthouse at the eastern end of the Singapore Straits. The business over with, Freddie decided against Jeremy's invitation to join his crew that night for a screening of HMS Defiant, starring Alec Guinness and Dirk Bogarde. The film was a Napoleonic saga of bravery on the high seas with lots of lashing and floggings.

Freddie had another kind of lashing in mind for that night; one that involved a brass bedstead and a certain young lady.

***

At that same moment, Jonny, Lee and Jannah were making their final plans to reclaim the statue of Guan Yu. The statue was hidden in caves at Sialang about five kilometres south along the coast from Berakit, the site of the insurgent base. Apart from stealing the statue they had to find a way to overcome or outwit the pirates who stood guard. They realised that clothed in their black outfits, they could be mistaken for members of the pirate gang as their colour was the same as the 6-6-6.

In the 16th Century, the pirates cloaked their fleet in black sails and rigging. During an attack the pirates would blacken their faces, rendering them practically invisible for night attacks on English and Dutch merchantmen. They were skilful sea-robbers and over the years had successfully adapted to a changing commercial reality. The local population benefitted from smuggled contraband and so kept quiet about their black market activities. They lived side-by-side with the military who supplemented their meagre rations with a plentiful supply of stolen luxury goods.

The plan was for Lee's fighters to join the attack on the base and use it as cover. During the attack they would peel away and leave for Sialang. They would pass themselves off as members of the pirate gang and use the element of surprise to regain the statue. A high powered speedboat would be waiting to bring them back to Singapore. Simple. What could go wrong?

***

Billy, Alex and George moved like cats, soundless and lithe, stopping, waiting, then darting forward getting ever closer to the insurgent base, peering through night vision goggles to check the coast was clear. Alex kept a stopwatch on the perimeter guards, timing their movements. George was using an infrared heat seeking camera to locate possible entry points. Billy panned the base with an 8mm low light film camera.

It was three in the morning. The patrol guards were sluggish and inattentive, stopping to light cigarettes and sharing a few words as they passed each other. The guards in the high towers occasionally stamped their feet to keep their circulation flowing. Boredom dampened any desire other than to get back to the bunkhouse as quickly as they could. The familiar sound of waves breaking on the beach and smell of salty sea air were their predictable companions. They had no idea they were being watched by three undercover soldiers who were gathering intelligence, seeking out weak spots and planning a permanent exit for them from guard duty.

The base was surrounded by mosquito-infested plantations. The dense palms would act as excellent cover for the attackers if they approached from the landward side as all the Indonesian guns were pointing in the opposite direction, out to sea. Wire cutters would clear an entry point to allow access to the main weapon arsenal, after the tower guards and patrols had been eliminated. Stealth was the best approach of all.

The base boatyard was full of sampans all carrying fake Singapore maritime registration plates. Destroying these and putting the yard out of action would be a key objective. Alex and George took pictures of the rest of the base including the position of the briefing rooms and barracks. Billy made a special note of the command centre to steal details of safe houses and agent identities. Their work done, they slipped away into the night.

***

Arto Hakim's deception strategy was working. To date, he'd submitted two proposals that involved sowing mines but due to the age of the Soviet gifted minesweepers and the lack of replacement parts both plans had to be cancelled at the last minute. It was no coincidence that members of his crew had created a thriving black market in machine parts traded for Johnnie Walker Red Label and Rothmans cigarettes.

Arto made regular patrols to Berakit to take part in insurgent training exercises. These were becoming more and more frequent as his senior officers, members of the communist PKI - Partai Komunis Indonesia, were applying more pressure within the military hierarchy and pressing for more control. Arto heard rumours of possible action to tip the balance of power towards the communists and decided to keep a low profile. The next practice landing exercise for insurgents at the base was scheduled for the full moon. Arto's duties were to intercept sampans carrying trainee agents, and by doing so, teach them how to avoid being caught again.

Arto looked forward to these night manoeuvres. It was like playing war games in the dark.

Safe, predictable, enjoyable.

***

They were bathing in the afterglow. Their bodies locked together. Her back pressed tight against his chest. His face nestling in the curve of her neck, his hands caressing her breasts. Her hair sweetly perfumed with the fresh scent of mango and lime imprinting a memory forever in his mind. Their breathing even and measured now, resting from the pulsating excesses of their love making moments before.

Before Freddie, Jannah had never had sex with someone who put her needs first. Men wanted the experience of assailing her body, of gratifying themselves, of conquering then withdrawing leaving her unsatisfied, used. With Freddie, it was giving and taking as equals, each relishing the prospect of pleasuring the other.

Their lovemaking began with play before the foreplay. It was their no-contact time. Jannah would tease. She'd slowly let the towel she was wearing almost fall but not quite, catching it then deliberately letting it fall to the floor. She lay on the bed. Her hands massaged oil over her own body. Her eyes fixed on Freddie's naked body standing in front of her. Each watching the other.

The rules meant they couldn't get physical yet. Jannah caressed every sensitive part of her body. Finding her

G-spot and becoming more aroused by the electric darts of desire pinging up her body. Her nerve-endings fizzing like live wires waiting to explode. Her dancing fingers moving faster and faster. Her arousal becoming more and more intense as her wanton performance drove her toward the sublime, delicious point of climax, her eyes locked on Freddie, enticing, exposing, losing all inhibitions. Freddie watching, knowing the performance was a gift for him, seeing soft lips parting as her climax rocked her shuddering body. Freddie simultaneously joined her at the peak of orgasmic release.

Unlike their first beginnings when Freddie made love and Jannah had sex, this time they both came together in love. The intensity was given a sharper edge. They were keeping secrets from each other. Could this be the last time they made love?

Jannah knew about the raid, knew that Freddie was going into the firing line. For his part, Freddie suspected that Jannah had been briefed on the raid by Jonny Lau. He also expected Lee to be one of the 6-6-6 fighters. It followed that Jannah as a member of the inner circle would at least have an idea of the raid if not the precise detail. They both kept their secret.

If this was to be the last time together, Freddie was determined to make it unforgettable, to make the moment last. The bedstead was fashioned from antique French brass. The vertical bars were perfectly spaced for tying. It was Freddie's turn to imprint a memory for Jannah. A memory that she could recall and fantasise over, should he never return. It called for Jannah to be compliant and submissive. Freddie did not rush. Every move was deliberately crafted to heighten anticipation and maximise fulfilment.

Jannah moved to the centre of the bed, spreading her arms and legs wide. Freddie slid a pillow under her hips to lift her a few inches away from the satin sheets. One by one, he took lengths of wide red ribbon and strapped hands and ankles to the waiting bars. When the bonds were secure he kissed her deeply and applied a soft blindfold. He stepped back to allow Jannah's mind and body a few seconds to hang in the blackness of a sensory limbo. She lay in sensual darkness not knowing where on her body the first teasing kiss would be, where the first contact of his tongue would fall, when the gradual press of his body would settle and the blissful sensations as two easing into one would begin.

Desire heightened beyond ecstasy.

ELEVEN

Dusk 15th May 1965. Tanah Merah, East Coast Singapore. The Katong Irregulars Mustering Point.

Jonny Lau welcomed them, the cream of underworld enforcers. Each fighter nodded in respect as they entered the briefing room. Three or four from each of the major gangs, added to the six from the 6-6-6, produced a force of twenty. It was accepted that Jonny would select six of his best in honour of his organisation. No one guessed the real reason for the extra manpower, enough for two missions. The fighters were dressed like Ninja warriors in black with a sash on their left arm proudly emblazoning their individual gang motifs. Cody, Freddie, Billy, Alex and George wore jungle-green uniforms.

The three girls from Red Butterfly gang arrived last. They looked as though they'd been clubbing. They wore bright make-up, red lipstick to reflect their gang colour, skin tight outfits, their cleavages uplifted on eye catching show. The astute observer would notice that their high heels were replaced with black plimsolls - and the fact the girls were carrying machineguns. 'Ladies – dressed to kill I see.' Freddie greeted these friends with hugs and kisses. 'Gentlemen I'd like to introduce one of our diversionary tactics!' The girls did little bunny-hop dance moves in response to the intense interest of the men and from one man in particular. Cody was transfixed.

Jonny rose to set a sombre tone.

'Tonight, we will make history. We'll strike a blow that will be heard all the way to Jakarta and show General Sukarno he cannot play games with us or with Singapore. Tonight, we must put aside any rivalries and watch each other's backs. Good luck and safe return!'

The room went dark to be pierced by a beam of coned light from the film projector. Freddie explained the images. 'This film was taken by our SAS reconnaissance mission. Here you see our proposed landing spot and route through the palm plantation behind the Indonesian base. The ladies from the Red Butterfly will approach the main entrance and distract the guards. Our tactics are designed to avoid a full scale fire fight. Our strength lies in our martial arts skills. We are up against soldiers who will use their basic training in weaponry. We must out-think and out-manoeuvre them. The aim is to put the base out of business. This means our targets are to destroy the physical structures and training capacity. This is to be a surgical strike, a quick in and out, with the minimum of casualties.'

Freddie ran through the gang assignments:

'Red Butterfly: Guards and guard towers to the front of the compound: incapacitate or eliminate.

6-6-6: Command and control building to retrieve intelligence on their insurgent deployment in

Singapore and mainland Malaya. Then set charges to destroy the building.

Ang Soon: Boatyard, quay and launching ramps and all marine craft, sampans, launches and rubber boats - destroy.

See Tong: Armoury, munitions and explosives – destroy.

My team will provide cover and assistance where and when required, plus we'll be on hand to take delivery of intelligence documents.' Freddie had been pointing at the different targets as they appeared on a slide screen, photos courtesy of George.

Freddie continued. 'You will have the latest in night vision technology which amplifies light from the moon, stars and sky-glow giving almost daylight clarity. Use the sight to pinpoint targets and approach with stealth to silence the enemy, ideally without firing live rounds.

We'll be getting underway at midnight, to be in position for the attack at 0200hrs. Thank you.'

**

'Ten-Shun!' Arto Hakim's crew came to immediate readiness as the well-drilled and disciplined crew they were. 'Gentlemen, tonight we have the honour of being joined by Commander Oleg Rozanov of the Union of Soviet Socialist Republics Navy to witness our war game exercises at the Bintan training base. He will observe our methods and make a report on your performance.' Arto shook hands with Oleg and invited him to inspect the crew. Oleg had assumed the rank of Naval Commander for the purposes of this goodwill trip.

Arto explained their role in tonight's exercises. 'It's like a game of British Bulldog at sea. The insurgent sampans are tasked with attempting to land on the beach of Pasir Panjang that lies round the headland away from the Berakit base. Our job is to intercept them. A red flag is flown from the sampans that we capture putting them out of the game. The sampans that succeed have to land on the beach. The agents have to make their way across the sand flats, past teams of waiting guards and into the dense undergrowth and finally to an inland staging area called 'Home', where they plant white flags to complete their mission.

At the outset, each agent will be given a backpack full of painted stones weighing 30 kilos. The colour and weight is checked at the end. They will have their AK47, loaded with coloured darts, as we do not want any unnecessary accidents. The agents use white coloured darts, the guards red ones. If you're hit by a dart you're out of the game. There is a time limit. The war games commence at 23.00hrs and end at 0.200hrs.'

'I take it that there is sufficient live ammunition in case of any disruption by something as insignificant as a battalion of Gurkhas?' Oleg questioned.

'Of course!' Arto responded with good humour. 'Our launch is fully armed at all times and the beach guards have second rifles loaded with live ammunition and our agents are given five rounds each, that have to be accounted for at the end of the exercise. However, aggressive action is normally confined to Borneo. This sector has been quiet during the Konfrontasi, so we are not expecting any disruption, as you call it.'

'But we must be forever vigilant, comrade. Perhaps we can speak privately before we cast off.' Oleg managed to turn the suggestion into an order. The two walked to the end of the jetty, away from prying eyes and listening ears. This gave Oleg a chance to inspect the second reason for his trip; to discover how the Soviet naval assets that included 7 destroyers, 12 frigates, 17 corvettes, 6 submarines, 21 torpedo and 12 missile boats, were being used by the Indonesian navy. He knew that the more modern vessels were being crewed by Russian sailors, but it was clear many craft had not left harbour in weeks, possibly months.

His eyes gave him the evidence: rusting hulls, green slime on harbour ropes revealed that the mooring lines had not been used. The inattention by sailors and a seeming lack of purpose told him all he needed to know.

He'd send a report to his superiors with the conclusion that the Allied naval forces combined with fighter squadrons at RAF Tengah with their English Electric Lightnings, Gloster Javelins and Hawker Hunters, had kept the Indonesian navy locked-up in port.

Oleg made this walk to the end of the jetty to speak to Arto on a much bigger issue. 'Arto we've kept in touch since our first meeting, the day I joined the Singapore bureau. I've heard rumours about increasing friction within the army, the rise of the communist PKI and their influence over President Sukarno. Have you heard anything?'

Arto was instantly on his guard, playing a good communist. 'No, the greater the influence of our comrades the better, we must do all we can to resist any pressure from right wing dissidents.' Oleg heard the words but didn't believe a word of it. More and more he believed that power shifts were taking place. He needed to be as nimble as a dancer to sense danger and opportunity.

***

'Comrades in arms – you must be joking!' Alex said what Billy and George were thinking. How could they as trained soldiers fighting for recognition and respect in their Canadian homeland, call this motley crew of criminals comrades? The best would be to use them as cannon fodder and make sure the three of them moved and fought as one man. As soon as the action started they would see what kind of comrades they really were, whether they were watching people's backs or stabbing them in the back.

Each gang of fighters had gone into a huddle to view the photos and make themselves familiar with their targets. Billy noticed that Lee's team seemed particularly intense. They were keeping their voices low and taking longer to study their instructions. He also noticed Lee keeping track of Billy's movements and shooting him frequent glances across the room.

'This is it,' thought Billy. 'The Tioman reckoning.' This would be an ideal opportunity for Lee to settle the score about Tioman beach for once and for all. A stray bullet in the heat of battle aimed in his direction, a pointed blade slicing through his heart, he was alert to the challenge, alert to the danger. This would be no gentlemanly duelling pistols at dawn. This would be visceral. One of them would not leave Bintan Island alive.

Billy got it all wrong. Lee kept looking across believing that Billy had somehow realised his team had an ulterior motive. Lee could feel Billy's eyes on him and kept looking across to make sure their whisperings had not been overheard and nothing given away about the statue mission. Lee's head was spinning in a maelstrom of emotions about Jannah and his mind was constantly on her. Billy was the least of his problems.

Lee's passions moved from polar opposites: from taking a lover's revenge against Freddie, to wanting to fiercely protect her and make sure she was safe; to demonstrate the depth of his love for her by sacrificing his own happiness, so she could be happy. When Freddie stood up to talk, when Freddie took command, he could accept his rival's leadership qualities; he could understand Jannah's attraction for his adversary in love.

Love was blossoming elsewhere on the eve of battle. Soo Ling of the Red Butterfly gang was returning Cody looks with interest. When she turned those eyes on Cody, they pulled him in as if lassoed by invisible tendrils rendering him helpless. He was a marked man. It was as if after years of hunting, of looking, of finding comfort wherever he could, he had stumbled, tripped and fallen for the one person on the planet who had the potential to complete him.

Lust at first sight was fast turning into something more serious. Soo Ling had the latest Mary Quant bob-cut hair style with a fringe that curved just above her eyebrows framing her flawlessly beautiful face. Cody watched her bee-sting lips as she spoke, not hearing the words but captivated by the way her mouth sensuously moved, continually changing shape and creating tiny dimples in her cheeks. She wore a Basque-like top in black with red ribbon shaping and lifting her divinely pert breasts. When she spoke to him she had this cute pigeon-English, the oriental timbre of her voice soft and feminine. This six-foot country boy from Idaho was reduced to mush.

Jonny Lau, Freddie and Michael Yeo were in deep conversation when a motorcycle despatch rider arrived in a hail of flying gravel. He leapt from his machine and sprinted up the launch jetty with a buff-coloured envelope in his gloved hand. He tore off his helmet and goggles and thrust the envelope into Freddie's hand. The messenger was from RAF Chia Keng, the GCHQ listening centre. The code breakers in the UK had cracked the Indonesian army ciphers and could read secret radio traffic.

'Sir! Top Secret for you from RAF Chia Keng. For your immediate attention.'

Freddie tore open the envelope. The message read:

Indonesian Naval Radio Intercept: URGENT

'Bintan base war games confirmed for tonight. Pasir Panjang beach 23:00hrs – 02:00hrs. Suggest you revise operation timing. Bring attack forward.

Good luck. G H.'

The warning came from Wing Commander Gareth Hughes of 205 Squadron. Freddie immediately understood its significance. If they left immediately they would arrive in time to see the Indonesian agents leave their base to join the military manoeuvres – and leave it open to attack.

'Everyone – timings changed – we go now!' Freddie gave the order; Michael Yeo cast off the lines and doused the running lights. Jonny leapt from the boat to the jetty with one last message for Freddie, smiling as he delivered it and watched Freddie's momentary quizzical reaction.

'Jannah wishes you a safe return!'

Jonny's parting gift was to reveal his control over Jannah. Freddie realised he was a pawn in a bigger game – but what game – to what end?

The boat's wake spumed into a white V-shape slicing through the water.

The adventure had begun. The game was in play.

TWELVE

22:30 hrs - 15th May 1965. The Berakit Insurgent Base, Bintan Island, Indonesia

'Let me explain our rapid departure.' Freddie addressed the troops as they huddled tight together in the central section of the launch. 'I received word from our intelligence people that our Indonesian friends are holding a series of war games tonight. The timing is a gift for us. They'll begin their exercises at 23.00hrs and are due to end at 0.200hrs. This means by leaving now we can hide by the small offshore Kaja Island, watch them depart and choose the best moment to attack.

Billy, Alex and George, explosives experts, will be accompanying the 6-6-6, Ang Soon and See Tong gangs respectively, to set charges and timers and allow twenty minutes to safely get back to the boat. And if the Gods are with us, we'll be on our way home before the fireworks start. Cody will give cover and support to the Red Butterfly girls.' Freddie turned to Michael Yeo and spoke again. 'While we're waiting and watching - we'll disappear from view, here's our Captain.'

Michael Yeo stood up with some wooden poles and a sheet of material in his hands. 'It's amazing what you can do with bamboo and pieces of black cloth. At the island, we won't be a boat – we'll become a Kelong.

Along the shoreline of Kaja Island there's a series of Kelong fishing huts. By changing the shape of our hull with straight poles strapped together in a rectangular shape and draping the poles with black gauze we will look from seaward as if we're another fishing hut silhouetted against the beach. The poles will be high enough to cover the black rubber boats tied to the roof of the launch. We'll be able to see out though the gauze without being seen. When we get the command, our disguise will be thrown overboard and we'll become a lethal fighting vessel again. You'll go ashore and take your positions, ready for the girls to distract the guards and for the assault to begin.'

Cody was enjoying himself. He'd adopted the Red Butterfly gang in totality and Soo Ling especially. They squeezed together, flirting, laughing and joking with no thought of what was about to happen, partly because they were having a good time, and partly because they knew how to switch their brains from lover to fighter in the seconds it took to draw a breath.

Freddie looked at the fighters around him in the process of smearing stripes of black and green camouflage cream on their faces. Some expressionless, keeping their thoughts, worries and plans to themselves. Freddie was surrounded by caged tigers, killers who prowled the city streets. Would they follow his commands? Would they turn on each other when the fight was won? He was sitting on a powder keg of human brutality and realised he had to show by example that he could be as merciless to earn their respect. Freddie glanced up at the moon.

What did they call it, a hunter's moon? The moonlight glinting on the waves helped them steer their path to the uninhabited island of Kaja, to assume their disguise.

If Freddie had taken a little bit longer to gaze at the moon he would have seen, high in the westward sky, wisps of stratus cloud forming mares' tails, so called because they looked like the thin tangled strands of a horse's tail. Maybe he would have felt the wind on his cheek, chill and strengthen. Perhaps he would have read the signs and recognised the harbingers of a coming storm. He didn't. You can forgive him. His mind was on the here and now – not on what was coming next.

Inside the base an unsuspecting hour passed in lively activity. At first, commands were shouted and troops ran to their posts, bright lights shining, marine commandos with rifles jumped into sampans, diesel engines coughed smoke, cast off, gathered in convoy for the short trip to the assembly area in readiness for the games to begin. The base guards were oblivious to the row of binoculars watching every move. Finally, lights were dowsed and normality and quiet returned to the base.

Silently on board, the Singapore Defence Force launch, the bamboo and gauze had done their job and the make believe kelong floated to shore. Engine pistons rose and fell, propellers turned as the launch slowly paced its way to the landing beach.

The attack had begun.

***

Arto looked forward to the evening's sport. He saw the leading lanterns glimmer as sampan after sampan slipped by the headland. 'Ready? Full steam ahead! Let's teach these novices a first lesson in survival!' Arto made sure Oleg was wearing his life-jacket. 'Hold-on tight, Comrade: I hope you don't get seasick!' Arto's launch was in darkness, cutting through the waves at twenty knots and aiming straight for the stately procession of sampans bunched together. The launched cleaved through them, slicing the procession in two, bow waves crashing against sampans, spilling crews overboard. The small boats rocked, took on water and nearly capsized.

Arto turned a circle, switched on his million candlepower searchlight and drifted back to the sampans. 'If we were the Royal Navy you would be dead - not just soaking wet! Let this be your first lesson. Expect the unexpected and never assume anything, never show a light and keep vigilant!' Arto's crew helped the bedraggled swimmers on board and ceremoniously pinned a piece of red cloth to their uniforms. 'You're out of the game. Consider yourselves prisoners of the British or Australian Navy!'

While he was talking, Arto noticed with pleasure that a few of the sampans, showing initiative, had eased away from the blinding searchlight and begun their attempt to reach the beach. 'By the way, those of you that are still here, are sunk! You're prisoners too! You have to be as devious as the enemy. You've been caught and will pay the price with more training, because you are not safe to be let loose in Singapore or Malaysia! My crew will take your names and issue you with red loser's flags. Return to base immediately; that's an order!'

Oleg was delighted. 'That's what I call entertainment. Congratulations! I will send a glowing report to your superiors. Just one thing, I thought you said the teams were using coloured darts to strike their opponents, I may be wrong but that sounds like live ammunition being used?'

'Aaah, sometimes they switch to blanks or live rounds to simulate real conditions. Don't worry comrade, I'm sure everything's under control.' As soon as the words left his mouth, his brain violently disagreed. They WERE live rounds, but where was the crack of gunfire coming from?

***

The guards on the main gate had been on duty for six hours without a break. They were counting the minutes to being relieved. They'd settled back to the usual routine after the boats had left for the war games. Bored. Tired. Hungry. The surreal vision of the Red Butterfly girls seemed to appear from nowhere. They giggled and waved, calling out: 'Hey Mr Soldier! Can you help us lost little girls?' Not surprisingly, logic and reason took second place to the flesh and blood images standing right in front of them. This was no mirage. This was too good to be true.

This was the signal for wire cutters to eat through the perimeter fence as the teams sprang into action. They moved with the fluidity of rolling mist to take up their positions, silencing wandering guards with killer bolts from crossbows, throwing knives striking with deadly accuracy or the graceful finality of a broken neck and a snapped spine courtesy of these supreme martial artists. Many of the guards were transported from the real world to the afterlife with only a bemused, quizzical look on their faces. Billy, Alex and George directed silenced sniper fire at guards manning the high towers with their Remington 700 bolt action rifles with Surefire silencers and fitted with Starlight scopes. Pinpoint accuracy, silent and deadly.

All was going to plan until Cody made a mistake.

He mistimed his entrance. The girls were superlative, doing their job brilliantly. Three guards clustered around them within their easy reach a perfect striking distance. The girls teased and egged them on, encouraging them to move closer and closer. Cody watched as the girls took a step back in unison as if they had rehearsed the move a hundred times. They unleashed a violent frontal attack with kicks to the groin and karate chops to the throat. As the guards fell choking to the ground, another stepped from the guardroom. He froze momentarily, not understanding what was happening. Then his training kicked-in.

The guard raised his weapon and fired at a massive figure clad in jungle green and armed with a submachine gun. The bullet ripped through Cody's left shoulder, the searing heat piercing skin and glancing bone, slamming him backwards onto the tarmac. More guards came running. The alarm blared a warning to the soldiers still on the base. Camp lights blazed with the brilliance of daylight, blinding attacker and defender alike. All hell let loose. The girls grabbed their M16s hidden in the bushes and ran for cover. Cody scrabbled on his belly to the palm trees, the order from his CIA Station Chief ringing in his head 'Don't get caught, don't get caught.'

Soo Ling turned to see a pool of blood, a gun, but no sign of Cody.

'Fuuuck!' Cody's stream of invective transformed a word of one syllable into a bellowing scream, of annoyance, of frustration, of stupidity, that expended a whole lungful of his precious breath. The bullet caught him high on the shoulder muscle, entering and leaving by a neat round hole and embedding itself in the trunk of a palm tree. Cody pulled a padded bandage from the pocket of his combat trousers with his right hand and pressed it against the wound to stem the blood flow. Still shivering and trembling with shock, he managed to get onto his knees and looked back to the open and defenceless main gate. Inert shapes lay rigid on the ground, arms and legs twisted at obscene angles, their spirits having fled to the safety of another, kinder realm.

The remaining guards had been caught cold, they were so used to living a quiet life they had no notion of fighting a vengeful enemy. Their officers were the first targets of the assassins in black.

Conventional military responses were no match to the silky killing skills they faced. They had no answer to the speed and accuracy of attack that had them spinning in leaderless chaos. Each gang had cleared a path to their assigned area.

Billy, Alex and George set their explosive charges while being protected by their gangs who'd switched to M16s to counter incoming rifle fire. The Red Butterfly girls joined the 6-6-6 and Freddie for their assault on the command and control building.

***

Arto gave orders to cut the engines and for the crew to keep silent. His practised ears picked up the immediate sounds of the commotion on the beach. The triumphant shouts from the catchers mingled with the curses from those caught before they reached the staging area. His ears also identified the crack of blank or live rounds along the shoreline, but it was the distant rumbling that prompted him to swing his binoculars over towards the headland to Berakit. The cloud layer above the base reflected a dimpled glow of red and orange from the ground. He could also see a smudge of black smoke spiralling upwards.

Arto tried to contact the base. The empty crackling static, the lost signal from his short wave radio confirmed his worst fears. The base was being attacked. They'd been outflanked. The only swift response options were the sampans that were returning to base after failing in the war games, and his gunboat. To make matters worse, the weather was closing in. Gone were the tranquil seas of an hour ago. Whitecap waves pushed by the ever increasing wind were chopping the surface of the sea, stinging spray whipped and sliced sideways. The Sumatra storm gathered strength to show what forces nature held in its armoury.

***

Jonny Lau had given explicit instructions for Lee to provide extra protection for Freddie. Lee assigned the two girls on the 6-6-6 team to this duty. The girls kept close to Freddie while Lee and the rest of the team led the assault on the command building. The Red Butterfly girls joined them, crashing into the operations room, guns blazing. The assault was over in minutes. When he was certain any opposition was either dead or vanished, Freddie began the job of ransacking filing cabinets for intelligence and tearing down wall maps and madly stuffing documents in his backpack. He was totally absorbed until a hand grabbed his arm and wrenched him away from his frantic task with surprising strength.

Soo Ling jerked him to his feet and shoved her distraught face right into his, close enough for him to smell her breath and feel the spray of her spittle. 'Cody's been shot!'

At the same instant George and Alex appeared at a side window. George shouting 'Clear to go boss, charges set and timers running'.

It was as if Freddie was being brutally pummelled in a boxing ring. The news that Cody had been shot snapped his head backwards from the face to face with Soo Ling. The warning cry of the imminent explosion was the second strike. Freddie was being dive-bombed with a multitude of simultaneous messages coming from every direction in the thick of battle. He was being stretched to the limit. His command training gave his mind an infinitesimal second to survive the dilemma, think clearly, and make his decision.

'Let's get out of here.' Freddie gave the order for all fighters to retreat to the beach. 'I can't leave Cody. I've got to find him.'

'You shouldn't speak ill of the almost dead!' Cody leant against a blood smeared doorframe, his left arm hanging uselessly by his side, the camouflage green and black sleeve drenched a muddy crimson red.

Freddie and Soo Ling rushed to give him support. They struggled with Cody's weight and staggered along like a giant mortally wounded stag beetle stooping and sliding, making relentlessly for the beach. The rain hammered down, slimy mud slipped under their boots with every squelching, gruelling step.

Billy set to work to arm his explosives. He made one final check on the explosives. Looking up he couldn't believe his eyes, Lee and his team leaving but going the wrong way. Not to the beach, but in the opposite direction towards the main gate, travelling south.

George and Alex yelled for Billy to get out and join them immediately, only minutes remained until the whole base erupted. Billy waved them away.

'You go boys – got some unfinished business – see you back in Bugis Street!'

Billy raced after Lee, running south, sprinting headlong toward his fate.

***

Above them, flying through the storm, Flight Engineer James Thomas called out with anxiety in his voice. 'Oil pressures dropping in Number Two engine.' The Shackleton's Griffon engines were thirsty for fuel, gulped oil and were high on maintenance. Wing Commander Gareth Hughes was in the left-hand seat.

'Thanks Jimmy, the weather's closing in too, visibility poor and wind speed rising. Navigator, set a course for the airfield.' His co-pilot radioed RAF Changi with their estimated time of arrival.

Gareth saw several flashes through the clouds at ground level. He banked the aircraft and turned for home with a leaving thought: 'Sorry Freddie – your babysitter has to leave you – all the best and good hunting.'

***

'We're not going to make the beach.' Dragging Cody through the mud, resting and crouching to avoid any gunfire, was sapping their strength and taking too long. Freddie had to create a Plan B or they would not survive. Being captured and interned before facing a firing squad was not an option. With less than eight minutes to go he had to come up with something fast. Then he saw it. The Ang Soon gang had done a great job wrecking the boatyard and quay. Sampans were smashed and sunk, all except one. The superstructure had been damaged but it was otherwise intact. The gang must have followed the order to retreat and figured the explosion would do the job they had no time to complete.

The two 6-6-6 girls hid behind 40 gallon oil drums giving covering fire before leaping into the boat to join them. Cody had turned the colour of ash. Soo Ling, with Shirani and Jenny Tong, the other members of Red Butterfly, covered his ice-cold body as best they could. Freddie primed and pushed the starter of the ancient diesel. Nothing. He tried again and got a pathetically weak coughing splutter. One last try and the engine caught. Freddie sprinted from stem to stern frantically throwing the mooring lines into the water. No time to check the fuel level, only time to live.

The explosives ignited with machinegun rapidity, wreaking carnage of end-of-the-earth proportions.

Bodies were blown to oblivion. Bricks, cement, metal towers, wooden structures, flying glass, every kind of debris and shrapnel scythed outwards levelling everything in its path.

A procession of shock-waves rocked the sampan. By lying flat and holding on for dear life, with the throttle wide open they managed to pull away from the jetty and make open water. They escaped a man-made hell to sail slap bang into a natural one. The power of the wind was worse than any Sumatra squall Freddie had ever seen. It was as if the sea was bitterly enraged at the wonton destruction taking place on land. The sampan was awash, the crouching bodies were soaked, each sheet of rain was hitting skin like tiny metal daggers stinging and driving into their bodies. The drenching overwhelming combination of rain and waves made it impossible to see anything in front of them.

Their blindness saved them.

As they made more headway against the current and prevailing gusts, they sailed straight into the middle of the sampan flotilla returning from the war games. As the boats were being buffeted and twisted with the wind-shear, rolling and tossing in the waves, it was easy to mistake an inward going boat with one going outward to the open sea. As Freddie's sampan was clearly from the base with its fake Singapore ID number plate in evidence, not a single shot was fired. Only when the wind eased and the visibility improved, did Freddie realise the magnitude of their luck and good fortune. By that time they were out of danger with a course set for the safety of Tanah Merah.

Michael Yeo had waited for as long as he could and could wait no longer. The Singapore Defence Launch had its bow into the wind and was riding the storm. His crew were pulling the exhausted, the wounded, the victorious fighters from the rubber boats until all were accounted for apart from Billy, Lee, the other three members of the 6-6-6 gang, Freddie, Cody, Red Butterfly and the two missing 6-6-6 girls. As the explosions ripped the sky, he gave the orders to start the engines and get underway, in search of safety.

***

Oleg was seasick green. He grabbed hold of the straps of his lifejacket in the hope that the harder he held them the safer he'd be. Arto was skilfully urging the gunboat through the peaks and troughs of the mountainous waves. The twin screws of his propellers left the sea completely when they crested the biggest waves. The engine noise screaming before the screws hit water again driving the boat forward. His mind was resolutely fixed on catching and passing the sampans to provide support for the defenders of the base. The gunboat was still in deep water off the headland when he heard the first blast, instantly followed by flashes and further shattering explosions. His attention and that of his crew was on the land not the sea.

120 rounds per minute of high explosive shells from the Bofors 40 mounted on the foredeck of HMS Fiskerton slammed into the stern of Arto's gunboat. The concentration and accuracy of the shots in those conditions was exceptional even allowing for the wild bucking in the storm. The shells chewed through the outer housing and disintegrated the rudder, ruining steerage and leaving the gunboat floundering and helpless. Jeremy Crawford ordered a final burst from

the twin 20mm Oerlikon cannon to spray a warning shot over the heads of the Indonesian gunboat to stifle any thoughts of resistance.

As Fiskerton came alongside the loud hailer gave the ultimatum. 'Surrender to Her Majesty's Navy. Heave to, lay down your arms, and lower your ensign. You will be boarded by Royal Marines, comply immediately to avoid any loss of life.' Captain Crawford ordered the Marines to board.

Arto offered no resistance. He gave orders to raise a white flag. Oleg could not have been happier; he was feeling like death warmed up.

They would live to fight another day.

THIRTEEN

04:00 hrs. 16th May 1965. Drifting in the Singapore Straits.

The engine sputtered and died. Fuel tank empty. Diesel gone, the last dregs of rust and grimy metal filings had been sucked from the bottom of the tank jamming the juddering fuel pump. They were drifting in the Singapore Straits, caught in the currents, blown by the wind, shivering with cold, exhausted, helpless. The waning moon was their only companion. Freddie knew Cody had only hours to live. He was deep in a black void of unconsciousness, far away from a world of pain, slipping ever closer to the end of life. The girls were huddled together, holding each other to capture what little body heat they could generate and direct it inwards like a troop of dishevelled and dispirited Emperor penguins.

The wind was abating and the waves began to languidly roll and settle, as if the anger of the storm had dissipated, like a truce after a lovers' quarrel. The sky was clearing too. In the distance a flashing light penetrated the darkness. Freddie thought he was hallucinating. He could barely keep his eyes open. He was feeling the after-effects of their lucky escape. His heart was no longer jumping out of his chest. At best it could only pump blood in lazy half-hearted pulses as his whole system neared shutdown. The distant light flashed and disappeared, flashed and disappeared teased his brain until it finally solved the riddle. It was the Horsburgh lighthouse on the rocky outcrop of Pedra Branca. The light gave him hope. They had to survive until sunrise, to survive another hour of torment, before the sun rose in the east. The morning sun was their only hope.

Freddie prayed that someone would be awake and alert on Pedra Branca.

***

Billy hung back in the chase not wanting to be seen. Ahead, the four figures moved at speed like ghostly wraiths going due south to Sialang. Billy's expertise in jungle craft made him almost invisible as he tracked the 6-6-6 team. Shafts of lightning pierced the cloud cover and illuminated the ground, picking out the runners as if they were flicking cells in a celestial film caught in slow motion action between blinding light and blackness. As they didn't expect to be followed, their focus was forwards, not backwards. Billy reached the top of a slight incline and looked down as another bolt of lightning split the sky and lit the earth. He saw the 6-6-6 team careering straight into an ambush.

Earlier, a few of the pirate gang had been playing cards, drinking, smoking, arguing and enjoying a quiet night. They were at the cave merely to keep watch and socialise, other members of their crew having gone to see their women or carouse with friends, as no attacks on shipping had been planned that night because of the storm. The muffled sound of persistent small-arms fire penetrated the cave. Their first reaction was to kick over the card table, spilling drinks, smashing glasses before reaching for their guns. The second was they weren't in danger, they weren't the target. For years they'd lived in quiet separation from the insurgent base. The soldiers were excellent customers.

They left the cave and followed the narrow path towards the base wearing their dirty oilskins as protection against wind and rain; oilskins that concealed them effectively in the dank undergrowth so that their bodies could be mistaken as boulders or fallen lumps of palm trunks to the onrushing 6-6-6 gang. Billy could see this inexorable collision as if he was witnessing a slow motion car crash, the momentum building by the second to reach the point of gruesome violent impact. Whatever his feelings against Lee he knew what he had to do.

The night sight of his Remington 700 picked out the leader. Lee's team flung themselves to the ground as one body then the next were punched backwards with the bullet's impact, killed by an unknown hand. Simultaneously behind them the insurgent base was blasted to destruction. The shock of the base exploding made one of the pirates get to his knees and reveal his position only to die in the mud by another dead shot from Billy's rifle. The last pirate stayed motionless on the ground playing dead. Lee signalled the team to move on. He looked back but there was nothing to see, no sign of their avenging angel.

***

The passengers and crew of the Singapore Defence Force launch gave a collective sigh of relief when they saw the lights of Tanah Merah blinking a welcome in the distance. Despite the storm they'd made good time. During the crossing, Michael Yeo with a heavy heart had kept a log of the attack from the time they reached Kaja Island to their return. Someone had to be able to report on the events of the evening, someone had to give an account of the objectives, keep a tally of the dead and wounded, and make an assessment of the annihilation inflicted on the base.

The report ended with the names of Freddie Burton, Cody Jackson, Billy Chang, Lee Jaya and three unnamed fighters all missing in action. Believed dead.

Each of the triad teams had people waiting to mend wounds, bundle them into cars and take them back to safe houses to eat, sleep and recover. Alex and George were met and taken back to barracks. No celebration. Getting back in one piece was enough. Michael Yeo checked in by radio to register their safe arrival, and asked for all search and rescue units to keep watch for any craft leaving Bintan waters. In fifteen minutes the jetty was empty, the launch was tied up for the night, floating peacefully at rest.

Jannah stood overlooking the jetty, her eyes hollow with grief. She began her solitary vigil with only one question in her mind. 'Were the two loves of her life still alive?'

***

It soon became clear from the water flooding into the bilge that Arto's gunboat would not survive. The order was given to abandon ship. Arto's crew and Oleg were taken aboard HMS Fiskerton. Captain Crawford took possession of Arto's secret code books and cast off the tow lines. Arto saluted as their boat disappeared into a watery grave, gurgling and belching shafts of air as it slid below the surface. Respect among fellow seafarers meant that rum, warm clothing and bowls of hot soup were provided and gratefully received.

One of Captain Crawford's officers entered his cabin. 'I think we've caught a rather strange fish in our net, Sir. Here's his ID. Oleg Rozanov, Economic Attaché, Embassy of the USSR, Singapore.'

'Hmmm, a strange fish or a big fish?' Crawford looked at Oleg's papers. 'Thank you Sub-Lieutenant. Show him in.' Jeremy Crawford sat at a desk in the wardroom by the aft bulkhead, one of the few places big enough on a Ton class minesweeper to hold a private meeting. He occupied himself leafing through some papers until he sensed Oleg's presence. He continued to concentrate on the papers long enough to make Oleg wait for recognition and appreciate the intended disrespectful slight.

'Wrong time, wrong place, Mr Rozanov? A war zone must be a strange location for an economic attaché.'

'Indeed, indeed Captain, I was unexpectedly caught up, through no fault of my own. I was on my way to a meeting to discuss grain yields when the fighting started and Captain Hakim was diverted to Berakit.' Oleg played the innocent, a mere office clerk unaccustomed to high adventure.

'I'm sure that's exactly what happened – wars can be so damned inconvenient!' Jeremy's sarcasm flew over Oleg's head like a flock of squawking seagulls. 'Someone is bound to want to have a chat with you when we get back to Sembawang. They shouldn't detain you too long. Our medical officer will give you something for seasickness.'

Oleg was dismissed. Next, Captain Crawford called for Arto Hakim.

'Captain Hakim, my crew has heard your crew talking. This has revealed some important information.' Arto was immediately on his guard, scared of what had been given away to the enemy. 'It seems they hold you in high regard, as man and mariner. We may be on different sides, but in times like these, one has to acknowledge and respect the talents of our adversaries. You may be assured that your crew will be looked after when we dock, and will probably be returned to your homeland as soon as we are able. As for yourself, our security services will want an interview, and there's someone there I would like you to meet. We will talk again in Singapore. You may rejoin your men.'

***

Meanwhile back in the undergrowth...

As soon as the coast was clear the pirate who'd played dead lifted his head, got on his haunches and sped off as if the very devil was on his tail. He was right. He was. Billy had seen him rise from the undergrowth and reasoned he would lead him directly to his hideout to raise the alarm. Billy was spurred on by the feeling that something important involving Lee and 6-6-6 was going on but he had no idea what it was or where he was being drawn to by the runner. All he knew was that Lee's team had fought valiantly alongside the other street gangs and completed their assigned mission before they broke away to go it alone.

That was enough for Billy to become their mysterious guardian - at least for now.

Every pirate cave has a secret entrance. The Sialang caves had several. Each cave had dark winding passageways memorised by the pirates and never divulged to outsiders. Only after a pirate had proved bravery and loyalty would he or she would be initiated to learn by heart the places where their bounty of gold and precious stones, of priceless relics and long stolen treasures were hidden.

Their everyday trading contraband, barrels of rum and cognac, cigarettes and cases of whisky were piled high to the curved and dusty ceiling close to the entrance where commerce could be conducted with ease. Further back were held the armaments. Boxes of rifles, machine guns, explosives and ammunition were stacked in neat rows to sell to the highest bidder no matter what grievance or terrorist cause they represented.

The fleeing pirate vanished. Billy had used all his stalking skills to follow without giving himself away. The trail went cold. He approached the last sighting and used the infrared gun sight to scan the ground. In his headlong flight the pirate had not concealed the hidden entrance properly with palm fronds. Billy spotted a chaotic pile thrown together, he pulled them aside to reveal a steep vertical drop into darkness.

Lee and his team reached the caves and took up observation positions. This was where their information dried up. They had to decide their point of entry and hope they'd picked the right cave to lead them to the statue. In the same way that the raw wildness of nature had smiled upon Freddie, helping him make his escape among the returning sampans, the tempest had come to their aid with the fury of wind and spiralling sand torn from the beach slamming against the cave entrances, forcing the guards to seek shelter and safety inside. Covering their faces and stooping with the wind at their backs, Lee and his men in black reached the caves without mishap.

As they crouched, steeling themselves to attack, a door bleached white and cracked with age, creaked open wide enough for a hand, wrist and arm to gingerly push outwards. The arm was followed by a scarred and pockmarked face that only a mother could love. The face turned left and right to check all was well. The arm went from being comfortably attached to the shoulder to being wrenched and dislocated with agonising ferocity. The rest of the body, including the grizzled head was twisted and pitched onto the ground by two ninja warriors. 'Take us to the statue of Guan Yu - or die. We want the statue, nothing else'. Lee dragged the guard to his feet to become their human shield. The 6-6-6 team pushed through the door and cautiously entered the cave.

'Friend of yours?' Billy was on his knees, hands tied behind his back, blood streaming from the deep cut on his head. A pistol pressed to the base of his skull in execution mode. The pirate leader Seto Kurnia was flanked either side by his men. The pirate to his left was wearing his oil skins, covered in mud and dripping wet. The pirate to his right pointed his machine gun with the safety catch off.' We caught this rat in a trap; it seems we are in an equal trading position. You have my man and I have yours.'

'Not quite.' Lee looked at Billy as if he was something disgusting stuck to the bottom of his shoe. 'The scum you're holding is not one of us. Does he look like us? Is he wearing the black of our fighters? Has he got a gang armband? He is nothing to do with the proud traditions of the 6-6-6.

In fact, you've done us a huge service by capturing this killer. He is nothing, a steaming pile of shit.' Lee continued staring directly into the eyes of Seto Kurnia wondering who would blink first.

'Shoot him now if you want, and be rid of him. But business comes first, I need to reach into my jacket to get a leather pouch of diamonds, don't shoot, I'll put down my gun.' The word diamonds got their attention. 'We're here to trade not to fight.'

Seto looked like a central casting pirate. Tall, muscular build with a red vest and beaten and creased brown leather waistcoat, hair tied back in a ponytail, sharp intelligent eyes, tattoos on his forearm and signs of healed cuts and scars gave testament to his line of business. His stock in trade happened to be stolen goods and creating mayhem. Underneath the intimidating exterior was an equally shrewd and intimidating interior.

'So, you're Jonny Lau's boys. That means I'll take you seriously, as long as you show me respect. We are really one and the same – pirates. We're pirates of the sea – you're pirates on the land. We both exist outside the law. We're both criminals and both in the business of crime. You're here because the Indonesian military is hitting your bank accounts by scaring off your customers for women, drugs, protection and gambling. Out with it, what do you want so much that you've joined the attack to get here? This has Jonny Lau's scheming written all over it.' Seto Kurnia read Lee's reaction and knew he was on the right track.

'The statue of Guan Yu, the God of War is the symbol of the 6-6-6. It was stolen long ago. It's time for the statue's honourable return. I hope we can come to some suitable arrangement; flawless diamonds for our statue. We know it's here.'

'Well I guess everything has its price.' Seto was unexpectedly compliant. Was it because many of his crew were not there? He knew that some of his men had been killed; although he didn't know if Billy was the killer or the men standing in front of him were responsible. Was he playing for time?

Lee poured a shower of glittering diamonds from the pouch into his hand. 'These diamonds are valued at one hundred thousand dollars at current market rates.' Lee tipped the diamonds back into the pouch and dangled them temptingly in the air.

'I can see Jonny has considered this offer carefully, to allow for both the cash value of the statue and an added extra to recognise its symbolic value. Diamonds are a universal currency, this shows good faith too. It is not every day I'm made such a rich proposition.' Seto drew breath. 'But there again, I would lose face if I accepted a first offer. I need a richer reward to part with something that has been in our possession for over one hundred years, don't you agree?'

Lee slipped his hand into another pocket. 'Jonny thought you'd say that.' He withdrew a clenched fist and extended his forearm. Lee's fingers moved slowly like the tentacles of a sea anemone opening by tiny degrees. Cupped in his palm was the biggest single sparkling diamond Seto had ever seen, a diamond of flawless, exceptional beauty. 'A 35 carat diamond, valued at over two hundred thousand dollars. It's our final offer.'

Lee said the last four words slowly with particular emphasis. The words were uttered with an underlying threat – accept or die. 'A fair exchange, give my regards to Jonny.' Seto agreed to the exchange. The deal was set, anxiety eased and mirrored in the body language as opponents relaxed. Seto gave the order to one of his men. 'Irawan, please fetch the statue.'

While all the attention was on the statue negotiations Billy had the chance to loosen his wrists behind his back. He kept them in position but was ready to loosen the ties whenever the opportunity arose. Billy was alert in every fibre of his being. His captor was looking towards his leader while still pointing a gun at Billy's head. As Billy was being held at the back of the cave, he had a better view of the tunnels that led off from the cave entrance. He saw Irawan returning with the statue before Lee and his boys saw him. Billy realised the 6-6-6 boys had let their guard down, getting the statue back without a fight was a massive triumph for them. Lee was standing slightly apart, holding the diamonds. His team stood grinning at each other. Billy's heightened senses picked up movement behind Irawan.

A movement of guards with guns locked and loaded.

'LEEEEEE!' Billy's warning cry reached Lee at the same time as two heads belonging to Lee's men exploded. Hair, bone and brains flew through the air, face grins still in place. Lee fell to the ground rolling and firing. Seto caught a bullet in the throat just under his chin, exiting through the top of his skull, lifting him off the ground with legs kicking in spasms. Billy, freeing his hands, grabbed a weapon and began shooting. His first victim was his captor in dirty oilskins, his blood mingling with the dirt and wet of his jacket.

The surviving 6-6-6 fighters shot into the tunnel after Seto's men, Irawan's retreating back exploded, thrusting him forward, the statue falling from his hands and cartwheeling in the dirt. The red mist of battle transformed the 6-6-6 fighters into men possessed, screaming like banshees, inflicting unspeakable retribution, bloodlust powering the outraged killing machines they'd become. Leaving broken bodies in their wake.

The intense sound of gunfire in such a confined space was beyond endurance. The acrid smoke of firearms being discharged, mixed with the pungent smell of burnt gunpowder, hung as a swirling fog of war inside the cave. When the firing stopped it was impossible to hear anything but the tortured muffled deafness in damaged eardrums. Lee picked up the diamond pouch and called to his men to get out.

Billy was nowhere to be seen. 'I think this is yours.' He was waiting outside the cave with the statue safe in his hands. The passing of the statue from one equal to another sealed and closed the past. In future, they would be brothers in arms.

Seto Kurnia's powerboat waited at the dock, bucking and kicking like a tethered stallion in the storm. A rich man's toy not designed for dicing with death in a raging tempest.

***

Dawn in the Singapore straits came and went. The sun rose and gained strength. The Horsburgh Light was a distant spot on the horizon. No one spotted them. No alarm was raised. No rescue.

Freddie was slumped over the tiller, his body submitting to the sweet siren call of sleep. The sampan was silent, bodies lying in a jumbled heap, sheltered against the rising heat. Cody's pulse was an almost imperceptible blip.

The sampan started to roll violently from side to side. Spray splashed their faces. Freddie trapped inside slumber was reliving the storm in a baleful dream. He called out from within the vivid fits of hallucination: 'No enough, enough.'

HMS Narwhal, a Porpoise Class diesel-electric submarine surfaced, its wash lifting and bouncing the sampan like a rubber duck in a bath tub.

'I.V.-Saline drip for this one. Thank god he's wearing his Vietnam dog-tags, blood group O.'

Freddie felt strong arms lifting him and voices speaking softly a language he understood. His sore and blistered lips painfully parted to accept delicious, ambrosial drips of clean cold water, before passing out.

The girls slept on, safely cocooned inside the belly of a giant metal whale.

FOURTEEN

10:00 hrs. 16th May 1965, FEAFOC Operations Room, RAF Changi.

No one spoke. Heads were craned upwards to study the before and after reconnaissance photographs blown-up and stuck on the wall. Photographs that were taken with the twin exposure F97 camera fitted in Avro Shackleton MR2's. The principle was to have two cameras firing the shutters independently at regular intervals to create one scrolling panoramic image, created by overlapping exposures. The before image showed the Berakit base in sharp outline. The quay, perimeter fence, the neat dormitories, and sturdy operation buildings were captured in exact and uncaring clarity. The after picture was of total desolation, as if an atomic bomb had struck and destroyed every living thing with clinical accuracy. Buildings flattened, the quay destroyed, the flotsam of death and destruction floating in the sea.

'Did we know about this?' The Air Marshal in command of FEAFOC had allowed only his most trusted officers to witness this carnage. 'Do we know who is responsible? Speak up.'

Wing Commander Gareth Hughes took a deep breath and responded. 'Sir, we were on our routine patrol over the Riau Islands last night when we developed engine trouble and had to return to the airfield. This must have happened during the storm after we'd left that sector. To answer your question, we don't have any further air intelligence at this time, apart from the recon photos you see.'

'Was there any army activity, any special ops, what about navy? I need to know what's going on here and fast. On the face of it the demolition of the Berakit base should be good news, but I want to know more before we start hanging out the flags and blowing trumpets.' The Air Marshal was wearing a hole in the carpet striding back and forth.

'There was an encounter off Bintan involving HMS Fiskerton with an Indonesian gunboat, but we have no evidence it's connected to this incident. Also, we intercepted a message from a Singapore Defence Force launch that made landfall at Tanah Merah after running before the storm. We assumed it was a warning to shipping about the ferocity of the weather and a request to keep a look out for any vessels in danger in the Eastern Straits. Lastly, I believe HMS Narwhal went to the aid of a disabled sampan beyond the Horsburgh light.' The intelligence officer delivered these facts with a 'this happens regularly' tone of voice, not volunteering any link between events.

'Okay, we'll sit on this for the time being. No contact with anyone unless approved personally by myself. Any further developments - bring them straight to me.' The Air Marshal was left alone to ponder the destruction before him.

'Peter.' A voice he recognised made him turn round. It was the Head of the GCHQ listening station and

Freddie's controller. 'We need to dissociate ourselves from this situation publically. Privately, it was one of ours; it was a complex mission of the most subversive and damaging kind to us, if ever the truth came out.

Take my advice and feel pleased that Singapore is now a much safer place. Don't ask awkward questions and give this incident your most cursory attention. These things happen in war and leave it at that. I'm working on an idea to give credit to a very deserving group of people. I promise to keep you, but only you, in the picture.

I must go. There's a couple of gentlemen I need to see in Sembawang.' The head of the secret service left as silently as he arrived.

***

Freddie lay in clean, crisp, perfectly white hospital sheets with a soft pillow for his head. He was faced by white walls, white blinds, and even a white T-shirt with a boy inside it. Chris was sitting in a white rattan chair. 'Freddie, I've seen you looking better.' Chris offered Freddie a glass of water and sat down. 'I've had the bandages removed from my hand after my firework accident. I was here for my final discharge and heard you were here. You're in Changi Hospital and I think Cody's recovering in intensive care. Whatever you guys have been up to must have been one hell of a party.'

'Cody's pulling through?' Freddie was up on his elbows, thanking every healing spirit in the known universe for this fantastic news.

Chris continued. 'Yeah, I heard the doctors talking and they said that he'd be dead without that blood transfusion. He needed four pints to fill him up. Apparently you were brought here after an emergency landing at Changi Creek. You came from a submarine or something, can't believe that, awesome!'

'What about the girls?' Freddie's memory was gradually filtering back.

'Girls! Freddie that must have been some night out! I know about boat trips to Pulau Ubin, but that's ridiculous!' Chris was in genuine awe. 'No, no girls around, just you and Cody.'

'Mr Burton, you're wanted. I'm afraid you have to get dressed. You have to leave for the Naval Base immediately.' The ward sister delivered the order and was gone, her heels beating a staccato retreat down the echoing hospital corridor. Freddie gingerly reached for his clothes. His body was trying to follow his brain's instructions, but Freddie was in a daze, mentally adrift on an ocean of questions.

'Chris, get me some paper and something to write with. I need you to deliver an important message. There's twenty dollars in my trouser pocket, you must go right now.'

'For twenty dollars, I'm there already!' The white chair was suddenly empty, the flattened seat cushion was the only sign a boy in a white T shirt was ever there. Chris caught the next bus into town, in search of for a large wooden door, down a side alley, with a peep-hole carved in the head of a dragon.

***

Powerboats go fast in straight lines, on flat calms. Lee, Billy and the two surviving 6-6-6 fighters had been riding a bucking bronco for two hours. The agonising trip was like being inside a relentless fast-spin cycle of a washing machine. The trip inflicted more damage to their battered bodies than anything encountered on land. Somehow they made the jetty at Tanah Merah bumping, scratching, crawling along the line of car tyre fenders to tie up. Each one of them too exhausted to reach out for the mooring lines, totally spent. Jannah had seen them appear through the rain and spray. She ran down the jetty screaming, willing her shouts to spark some sign of life. They didn't. The trauma of the hellish crossing had been too much. The four fighters lay slumped in the bucket seats, sea water swirling up to their knees, heads and arms cut and bruised.

Lee's head rested on the steering wheel, a lump as big as a goose egg on his forehead. He was out for the count. The man beside him looked in a bad way too. His jungle green arms locked over his chest holding something in the tightest grip as if rigor mortis had set in. The two remaining 6-6-6 fighters started to stir. One vomited, giving back to the sea a stomach full of putrid salt water.

The other, realising he was no longer in the spin cycle, attempted to pull his pain wracked body onto the low jetty, he collapsed, half in, half out of the boat.

***

At Sembawang naval base, HMS Fiskerton had docked; officers, crew and prisoners left the ship and gathered on the quayside. Jeremy Crawford briefed Freddie and his MI6 controller to one side and out of sight. 'They've been put in separate interview rooms, Captain Hakim and Mr Rozanov. Hakim's crew are going to be treated to a supervised tour around the base. They will see our naval power for themselves; this will provide an effective warning to their masters on their return. They won't see anything remotely sensitive though.'

Jeremy lowered his voice. 'That was some attack in Bintan last night. I've seen some pictures of the raid. It could stifle any insurgency activity for months to come. Well done Freddie, good work.' He offered a brisk respectful salute and left.

'And thanks to you and the Fiskerton!' Freddie called after him. Having consumed several cups of coffee he was starting to feel much better, the caffeine having whizzed round his system to wake up both body and mind.

Freddie's controller spoke. 'Right, I'll leave them to you. When you're finished with Mr Rozanov we'll contact the Russian Embassy. For Hakim, there's a Panama registered merchantman leaving Keppel Harbour tonight to take Hakim and his crew back to Batam. I won't join you in these interrogations, keeping a low profile you understand. I believe we already have a productive relationship with our Russian friend via our CIA friends. Use this little matter of saving his life as the final twist of the knife in his recruitment process.

As for Captain Hakim, I believe he could be most helpful over the coming months, as his non-communist sympathies could balance any communist intelligence input by Mr Rozanov. They'd be two sides of the same coin. That's why I want them back in their home surroundings as soon as possible.'

Freddie had been thinking about the best way to place Oleg back into his normal circle of operations. 'Actually, I wouldn't want to make any formal contact with the Russian Embassy. We need to protect our sources and I've prepared something for him. Leave it to me. I'll speak to Oleg Rozanov first. I'll report later.' The two men shook hands and went their separate ways.

Freddie had been thinking ahead and had produced two items: a folder for Oleg and a suitcase for Arto. Freddie picked up the folder and turned the handle on the first interview room. Oleg was wreathed in a fog of cigarette smoke. The ashtray full of crumpled butts of Marlboro's, betrayed his fraying nerves. This was a first meeting for Freddie as Cody had made all the running with Oleg.

Oleg had adopted a flat mask of indifference as Freddie entered the room. A look that lasted a fraction of a second. The time it took for his eyebrows to shoot upwards in reaction to Freddie's first words.

'Cody says hallo.' What those three words really said was: 'I know you. I've seen you on film, I've seen the photographs, we have you under our control, let's get down to business.' Freddie laid the folder in front of him without looking at it. 'Captain Crawford told me of your on-board interview. I want you to repeat that to me now, describe the situation and tell me exactly what was said: go.'

Oleg took a moment to recapture the memory then started. 'I was shown under guard to the wardroom. Captain Crawford sat at a desk looking at some official papers, after making me wait to show he was top dog, as you English say, he then covered the papers and asked me what an Economic Attaché was doing on an Indonesian gunboat in a war zone. I told him I was on my way to a...'

Freddie cut in.

'Stop right there. Let me tell you what happened next. You were interrupted by a rapid banging on the wardroom door. One of his crew rushed in with an urgent message from an officer saying trouble had broken out with the Indonesian gunboat crew. Captain Crawford immediately got up and left the room leaving one guard to keep an eye on you. The guard knowing you were unarmed, was more concerned with what was happening in the mess and kept looking out the open wardroom door. Captain Crawford in jumping up quickly from the desk had scattered the official papers on his desk. And this is what you saw...'

Freddie pushed the folder over to Oleg. Top Secret – For Your Eyes Only was stamped at an angle in bright red ink. The headline below read: HEDGEHOG MKII ANTI-SUBMARINE PROJECTILE. Below the headline was the image of a mortar bomb with fins, an inset of technical specifications along with a full operational description. Freddie continued. 'Taking advantage of the confusion and the inattention of the guard you cleverly slipped the document inside your jacket and waited for Captain Crawford's return. When he came back, you were dismissed. The Captain gathered up the scattered papers, but because there were still many demands upon him, in the middle of a storm, with a boat full of enemy combatants, he didn't notice the secret document was missing. Understand?'

Seeing that Oleg had not caught up, Freddie explained further. 'In the last war, the Hedgehog was an extremely effective anti-submarine weapon. It fired a pattern of 24 mortar propelled bombs, creating an explosive net of depth-charges around a fleeing enemy submarine. The explosions ripped the submarine apart. What you have in front of you is the latest Mark II development of a smaller more manageable 12 mortar version that will be mounted in front of the Bofors gun of ships to fire forward. This new version can also be set at various depths so our minesweepers could set bombs to explode on the surface destroying insurgent sampans.'

Oleg took and folded the secret document. 'We have a car waiting to take you back to Singapore. When questioned, tell everything as it actually happened – just add this little extra to impress them. It will reflect well on you. Cody expects you to continue trading relations as normal. I'm afraid he's rather inconvenienced at present, and asked me to see you on his behalf. Before you go, Cody said to remind you of a new life on the other side of the Iron Curtain. The offer's still open.' Oleg smiled and made for the door. Freddie, having delivered this expertly crafted piece of misinformation left to collect the suitcase and meet Arto Hakim.

Arto was devouring a newly arrived 7th May copy of the New Musical Express. He read every article, examined every photo, and perused every advertisement. The Beatles were number one with 'Ticket to Ride'. Van Morrison's band, Them, were number five in the charts with 'Here comes the Night'. The Kinks were headlining a UK tour supported by the Yardbirds. In the States, The Rolling Stones, Tom Jones and Dusty Springfield had all appeared on the same Ed Sullivan Show. The jazz news was that John

Coltrane was recording his new album 'Ascension' to be released later next year. Herbie Hancock's new album 'Maiden Voyage' was expected out shortly. Arto was so immersed, he hardly noticed a man carrying a suitcase enter the room.

'Captain Hakim, pleased to meet you, I'm Freddie Burton.' Freddie extended his hand. 'I've heard a lot about you from Captain Crawford and he sends his good wishes. Your men are now relaxing. We've made arrangements for you and your crew to be repatriated this evening. A merchantman, the Sea Emerald, is casting off from Keppel Harbour and we've secured passage under a pledge of safety from our navy and air force to dock at Batam Island. These arrangements for your safe return have been gratefully accepted by the Indonesian authorities.' Freddie drew breath and changed the subject. 'Why the suitcase?' Arto looked at the closed case as if it held some trick or unexpected horror to mar the so-far-so-good news. He needn't have worried.

'From now, until you embark on the Sea Emerald, you are my guest. I refuse to take you for a meal, to drink Tiger Beer or listen to live music, with you dressed as member of the Indonesian Marine Corps.' Freddie's fingers sprang the suitcase catches. Arto lifted the lid. Sitting on top was a pair of Levi jeans was a blue denim shirt. On top of the shirt of a black Boosey & Hawkes b-flat clarinet in a case of scarlet silk lining, complete with the finest quality Vandoren reeds. 'We thought you might like try it out?' They climbed into a taxi. Sembawang disappeared in a swirl of exhaust fumes.

***

Jannah read and re-read the message from Freddie, delivered by the boy she remembered from the rescue on the yacht Galadriel. Her tears of thanks, of joy, spotted white salty circles on the paper smudging and making the ink run with relief. The short note spoke volumes.

'Baby -Tonight we're going dancing.'

Two crossed slashes of a pen, signed a single kiss.

***

Jonny Lau knelt alone in his office in front of the empty plinth. Six new candles waited to be lit, the statue of Guan Yu cupped in his protective hands. He placed the statue with infinite care on the plinth, reuniting them at last. Candlelight flickered a welcome home.

***

The Attic Folk Club was on the left-hand side and set back about 150 yards from the main road out of Changi Village. Freddie decided this would be a good starting point for the evening. Later they would go into town to the Golden Venus club at the Orchard Hotel in Orchard Road, before Arto changed into his uniform and rejoined his crew at Keppel Harbour. Afterwards Freddie would be free to see Jannah; they would go dancing, drink champagne and at the end of the night celebrate between the sheets.

The Attic Club had a set of outside wooden steps that led to the roof room. A white painted ship's lifebuoy with Attic Folk painted in black letters had pride of place centre stage. A boy-girl duo with acoustic guitars were playing and going down well with the audience with some Donovan covers of Catch the Wind, Colours and The Universal Soldier. Arto was soaking up the relaxed and smoky atmosphere. The sensation of enjoying the music, being away from the war and from the burden of command was sweet indeed.

Trad jazz was on the menu at Golden Venus. After a few beers, Arto took out his new clarinet and joined the local band who were running through some Kenny Ball numbers. Arto couldn't resist playing along with fellow musician Acker Bilk's Stranger on the Shore. Acker's massive 1962 hit was the first US Billboard number one for a British artist. Arto knew it by heart.

When the band left the stage for a fifteen minute break, Freddie decided it was time to go to work. 'This confrontation is not going to last forever. We suspect things are about to change. Our sources tell us that trouble's brewing at the highest levels between nationalists and communist factions. We'd like to be alerted to any developments. We're not asking you to compromise your position; you must continue to do your duty. We're looking to the future when these troubles are over. That's it, that's all.'

It didn't take long for a decision. 'How would I contact you?' Arto was looking to the future too.

The two said their farewells at the foot of the Sea Emerald's boarding ramp. Arto, having changed back into uniform, walked up the gangway without a backward glance, clutching his new suitcase, with a smile on his face.

***

They were locked in each other's arms. Not gently as lovers, but holding on, gripping, binding themselves together for fear they that if they let go they would never find each other again. Their eyes were closed in deepest sleep, both separately reliving the trauma of the last 24 hours in a series of vivid flashbacks.

The moving pictures in Jannah's mind saw her bone cold, waiting for long hours without hope, soaked to the skin and being whipped by a merciless wind. A phantom boat appeared through the storm with four dead bodies, battered and bleeding. Their broken bodies squirming, their mouths belched geysers of raspberry red blood. The horror cleared to see her hugging Lee for warmth and he not being dead at all, beside him was a man she didn't know. The man held the statue of Guan Yu as if his life depended on it. The horror returned. Where was Freddie, why wasn't he here? Was he alive or dead? Panic ripped her to shreds. Fear caused her body to jack-knife upwards in sleep, the spasm shocking her into screaming wakefulness.

Freddie was beside her. His own flashbacks plugged into his nervous system and rippled down his twitching body. His eyes careered wildly behind his closed eyelids. His eyeballs moved at a breakneck speed like silver balls inside a human pinball machine. He suddenly broke free to reach out to grab Jannah to stop the devil pulling him back into the hell of Bintan.

The horror eased and faded away to lie in wait until the next time they slept.

They embraced gently as lovers.

FIFTEEN

09:00 hrs. 18th May 1965, A Fond Farewell.

'It's everywhere. The Straits Times has devoted most of the front page to it, the Malay, Tamil and Chinese language newspapers have got the story and Radio Malaysia and Television Malaysia have contacted the Government asking for interviews.' The headline of the English language newspaper read: INSURGENT BASE DESTROYED – SINGAPORE STRIKES BACK! 'The place is going wild. It will soon be picked up by the world's media.

The question is what are we going to do about it?'

The Air Marshal scanned the massed gathering in the operations room. In response, faces looked questioningly at other faces that looked vacantly back. 'Now I know that your people weren't involved directly with the fighting, but does anyone know who did take part and caused so much devastation?' Silence and shuffling of feet. 'And assuming that the attackers must have been either from Singapore or Malaya where did they come from? And how did they get back undetected?' More awkwardness. 'Fine, I need your recommendations on my desk by twelve noon today. Dismissed!'

The Air Marshall called in the Head of GCHQ listening station at RAF Chai Keng, he at least would have something positive to say. 'I would suggest a little subterfuge, a dash of deception, a sprinkling of duplicity, hidden under a cloak of cunning deviousness. That would be my advice. In short, I think we should put on a show.' Freddie's boss was loving these machinations.

'A show, an entertainment, a theatre production – what exactly is being hatched in that warped mind of yours?' The Air Marshal didn't enjoy being played for a fool.

'It does involve professional actors. Actors that will be flown in this evening by RAF Hastings transports from Bombay and the Hong Kong film studios. You see, we need actors to pose as heroic members of the Singapore Vigilante Force. They will be paraded through the streets in an open-top bus with a marching band walking alongside and the Dragon Dancers in support. There will be speeches and fireworks in celebration. All this will create a frenzy of excitement and adoration from a grateful public. The actors will be drawn from different nationalities, brave Malay, Chinese, Tamil, and Asians; a wide cross-section of Singapore society as an inspired display of racial harmony. It will be a masterstroke, a brilliantly conceived piece of public relations. The actors will be fully briefed beforehand to put on a wonderful show. Afterwards, money will change hands, the actors will be driven back to Changi to fly out and never be seen again. All the credit will go where it is most deserved: to the Singapore Defence Force.

I have people on hand who will coach the actors in the parts they'll play. Off the record, I've already laid the groundwork with the Singapore authorities. They've been kept in the dark about who actually carried out the attack. I suspect they have their own ideas about who was responsible. However, they immediately saw the benefits and are prepared to go along with it. Do I have your permission to set the wheels in motion for this Saturday the 22nd?' The head of MI6 finally stopped talking.

'Go ahead. Keep this charade Top Secret. As far as everyone else knows, this is the real deal with true life heroes.' The Air Marshal reached for a copy of the Straits Times. He turned to the sports pages to find the cricket score.

***

At the 6-6-6 headquarters Lee and Billy were deep in conversation. Because Billy carried and protected the Guan Yu statue, the 6-6-6 team adopted him as one of their own and brought him back to Bukit Timah to recover from the raid. Before Freddie made it back alive, Jannah had kept a watch on Lee and bathed the goose egg sized bump on his head. With rest and careful attention the two men were gaining strength and had some important issues to lay to rest. Although they'd started at different ends of the spectrum, they had much in common. Lee had been striving for freedom and recognition in Malaya, fighting for the communist cause. Billy too had been fighting on behalf of his Chinese countrymen in Canada for greater recognition and acceptance. Each had done things in the struggle they regretted, taking lives for their respective causes. Killing was not personal; it was necessary for survival. An unbreakable bond was forged in the caves of Sialang.

Their recuperation was turbo-charged by the added ministrations of two Red Butterfly girls. Shirani was taking Lee's recovery personally. This stunning Tamil girl provided a new spark in his life. Lee was finally moving on. Billy and Jenny Tong had got acquainted under the covers, indulging some very private and personal therapy regulating each other's blood pressure. For his part, Jonny Lau ensured that Billy wanted for nothing. Without him, Guan Yu would still be locked inside an Indonesian cave. Alex and George had made several trips to Bukit Timah and were greeted as brothers and treated like kings.

***

Upstairs, Jonny Lau had called a conference. His confidant inside the police force had tipped him off about the victory parade. Jonny had to admit it was a masterstroke of manipulation. The meeting was to acknowledge and thank the other gangs and to agree to a period of calm so business could get back to normal. The close relations between the police and the criminal underworld meant that anyone who needed the truth behind the raid already knew that it had nothing to do with the Singapore Defence Force. The rival gangs approved the idea of giving the credit to the force. This would be good politically and create a valuable honeymoon period with the authorities for the gangs to carry on their activities unmolested.

***

'I need you to be there on Saturday, are you feeling any better?' Freddie was sitting by Cody's bed in hospital. 'How's the shoulder?'

'Stitched-up and ready to go, it's the rest of the body that needs a month on Miami Beach. Why, what's happening on Saturday?' Freddie had visited him every day and told him the story of their rescue. 'The doc said I'd be ready to leave as long as I did nothing strenuous like chasing girls for at least a week.'

'Okay listen-up, this is the plan. A troop of actors are going to play the performance of their lives posing as members of the Singapore Defence Force. We're going to be their drama coaches.'

'Whoa! Back up. Fake fighters? Run that past me again, but this time, explain what the hell is going on.'

Freddie started again. 'The plan is for the Defence Force to take credit for the attack on Bintan, even though they had nothing to do with it. This takes attention away from us and the criminal underworld. After a parade, the actors will leave the island having bathed the Force in glory. The whole Bintan episode will be swept under a carpet the size of Singapore and be forgotten.'

'Why didn't you say that before?' Cody was already dressed.

'Good, now we're late for the actor briefing. I think your boss is going to be there, he'll be pleased to see you're not captured or dead.'

'What it is to be wanted.' Cody gingerly took his first steps since his blood transfusion.

'Here's something to cheer you up.' Freddie handed Cody an invitation in beautifully flowing Chinese script with an image of Guan Yu in the centre. 'Jonny Lau's throwing a celebration party at the Dragon Club on

Saturday night. We'll go along after the curtain comes down on the victory parade.'

The two friends left the hospital, Cody blowing kisses to the nurses.

***

Twenty young men wearing dark blue berets, grey short sleeved shirts with epaulets and long khaki shorts with a thick webbing belt were actors in costume. They sat waiting for the pre-production rehearsal meeting to begin.

'Listen up, please pay attention.' Tan BoonTek, Deputy Commandant of the Singapore Defence Force was ready to start the briefing.

'First I would like to thank you for participating in this special one night only performance. You will be greeted as heroes tomorrow and represent the proud traditions of the Force. All you need to know is that you are playing a part in a film production and your skills as actors are highly valued. You'll see the same cameras and lighting crews as you would expect on a normal film set. Your role will be as a group of returning heroes. You've been specially chosen to represent the racial mix we are honoured to have among our ranks.

In the morning, you will be taken by Gharry bus to the meeting point by Clifford Pier and Collyer Quay, where you will board an open-top bus to take part in a film about a victory parade. The men and women of the Force will march alongside the bus as you wave to the adoring crowd. We do expect a good turnout of local people. Some will be professional film extras like yourselves. The filming will be a one-take affair per scene, the whole parade will go on for some hours. You will be served refreshments and food snacks throughout the day.

The route of the parade will be up the South Bridge Road along the harbour and eventually reaching the Padang field in front of the Supreme Court building by the Singapore Cricket Club. This is where the Victory rally will be held. You will be seated with dignitaries on a raised platform.

One by one you will be called to receive the Singapore Conspicuous Gallantry Medal. These medals are to be returned to me immediately after the filming finishes without fail. The film director will be taking shots of the Raffles Hotel and other famous landmarks as the film will be used to promote Singapore to an international audience.

When the speeches and medal giving ceremony are finished, you will rejoin your bus to be taken back to Serangoon barracks to change, receive your acting fees and be taken to Changi airfield for your flight out.

Thank you.'

Freddie and Cody watched the proceedings with straight faces as the first act in the make-believe drama drew to a close.

***

Downtown Singapore was getting dark on the Padang field. The construction crew were building the staging for the victory parade and award ceremony; they were setting up rows of theatre arc lights and running out cables to the electricity generators. Two extra construction workers had joined the crew unnoticed. The insurgents attached high explosives to the two scaffolding poles that took the weight of the main stage. They wrapped black and yellow warning tape around the bombs to make them look like electric plugs and fuses, in keeping with a busy event site. After they set the bombs, they innocently worked alongside the construction team, seemingly relaxed, blending in, and not drawing attention to themselves. When the foreman called for a tea break, the two simply sauntered away.

The two had read the newspapers, witnessed the euphoria, and felt the anguish of losing friends in the attack on the Berakit base. They'd been contacted by their controller and graphically told of the carnage. This was to be their revenge, their turn to strike back.

***

The Singapore Infantry Regiment Band had already tuned up as the heroes' bus arrived. Roads on the route had been closed and members of the Defence Force were forming up by the open-top bus and waited for orders. The actors had been practising smiling and waving. They noted the film cameras mounted on flatbed trucks, the producer and director using an old style megaphone to shout instructions. The bus was draped in Singapore flags and red, white and blue bunting. The crowds were gathering all along the route to cheer and wave.

The event crew were checking microphones and speakers. The backstage area had been cordoned off and a VIP tent had been erected for the distinguished guests, officials and of course, the actors. Next to the tent was a set of steps leading to the stage. The tent did a great job of covering the scaffolding poles that were wrapped in colourful black and yellow tape. There was a gap of a few feet wide behind the VIP tent backing onto the stage. It was through this gap that the site manager walked. He was a stickler for correctness, pedantic in the extreme. He liked everything to be neat and tidy. He had a habit of talking to himself as he made his inspection rounds.

'Bloody electricians! Why don't they ever clean up after themselves? What have we got here? This tape is not secure, this end's flapping about, doesn't look right, and there's no electrical fittings here. Better take a look, no, no wires coming out, I wonder what this is. OH! MY GOD!'

The bomb disposal team were quickly on the scene and disarmed the bombs. The Police took away the explosives and declared the area safe. This was so efficiently done that a casual onlooker, or shall we say, two not-so-casual onlookers, didn't notice any break in the rhythm of work and preparation. To them the timers were set and it was a question of getting a grandstand view of their death dealing firework display. They decided to get something to eat.

The bombs were replaced by two rectangular blocks of wood of the same shape and size, and covered in sticky yellow and black tape.

The trap was set.

***

'Are you sure you set the timers correctly, they should have gone off by now?' The Indonesians, Ade and Ridwan were standing by the sea wall, a safe distance from the expected blast. 'Ade, something's wrong, are you certain the detonator wires were connected securely? We won't get a chance like this again, we owe it to our fallen comrades. We must do our duty.'

Ridwan, the senior office, had given Ade the honour of setting the charges. A decision he was now regretting. They dare not fail. He made a decision. 'It looks like total chaos over there; we'll become part of the crew again and use all the excitement to give us cover. We'll check and reset the timings and be away. We'll meet back here in twenty minutes. Be careful, use all your training and be alert. Let's do it.'

The victory parade had received rapturous applause along the length of the route. The Padang was heaving with people desperate to see their heroes. After an hour of speeches punctuated by the marching band intervening with trumpets blaring and drums banging, the medal ceremony was coming to a close. The actors were performing as the seasoned professionals they were. Some playing being humble, others nervous, all as overawed soldiers out of their depth by being treated as heroes. Overall, it was turning out to be a very slick ensemble performance. Occasionally the actors took it in turns to look directly into the cameras to help the director frame close-ups. They noticed the production assistant with the clapper board chalk up the ever increasing scene numbers. The delirious crowd were being bathed in bright floodlight to capture some excellent reaction shots. As soon as the ceremony was over, the actors would all come together onstage for a final group shot waving a goodbye to the cheering masses. They would leave the stage like rock stars with the band playing, having given the performance of their lives.

The bus would be waiting to whisk them away to their payday and flight home.

The cameras would continue to roll – without ever being loaded with film. The show was for show and nothing else.

Freddie and Cody wearing their VIP Access badges, stood by the side of the stage. They were thoroughly enjoying this extravagant production of deception, while being alert as they constantly scanned the crowd and backstage area; waiting for some uninvited guests to appear.

Ridwan was right. The tumult was such that attention was directed to what was happening front of the stage. He spotted a space in the line of protective crowd barriers, a small gap, that if they turned their bodies sideways they could slip through. It did not occur to them until afterwards that this gap was an open door - a trap door that was locked shut behind them.

The VIP tent that wasn't there before and was now blocking the stage, gave their brains the answer to why the bombs had not exploded. Ade and Ridwan assumed that when the tent was being erected, the explosive charges or timers must have been disturbed in some way. Perhaps the tape holding the bombs had been knocked somehow. That must be the answer; the rigging of the tent must have caused the problem.

They walked nonchalantly along the gap behind the tent. They got closer and closer to the bombs. Their hands started to unwind the black and yellow tape.

They had company.

***

Tan Boon Tek of the Defence Force was pleased. The success of the victory parade had been beyond his wildest dreams. Not only had the ruse worked, but he'd recovered twenty Vigilante Gallantry Medals and apprehended two insurgents. It had been a fine day's work. The stage breakdown was in full swing, the film crew putting their equipment inside flight cases. The actors were in high spirits for a job well done and were glowing with pride for an outstanding performance. They joyfully jostled and tumbled into the bus, calling out to the driver to start the engine and get going for their long journey home.

In Bugis Street, the champagne bar in the Dragon Club was heaving. Billy, Lee, Alex and George, Jannah, Soo Ling, Jenny Tong and Shirani were on their second glass of champagne when Freddie and Cody arrived. Jonny Lau had laid on the most amazing buffet, showcasing the very best in Chinese cuisine. The two 6-6-6 girls and the two surviving men from the Berakit raid came over and joined the group. There was such a wonderful feeling of happiness in the room, everyone on their best form, laughing and joking, relishing the fact that they had accomplished all they'd set out to do and somehow managed to return alive to tell the tale.

The lights dimmed. Jonny Lau moved to the centre of the room where the statue of Guan Yu was draped with a scarlet and gold cloth embroidered with golden dragons. As he spoke he lifted the drape to reveal the statue in all its glory. 'Guan Yu has been returned to us. Our statue is beyond price. It is a symbol for us all. It is by your actions that Guan Yu has been reunited with the 6-6-6 and my pledge is that everyone in this room will forever have our gratitude and support.

Furthermore, that Billy, Freddie and Cody will henceforth become honorary members of the 6-6-6 and be held in great respect from this day forward.' A persistent phone started ringing in Jannah's office. 'I give you Guan Yu and the new members of our organisation!' A toast was drunk, everyone cheered and hugged each other. Jonny made a special point of first embracing Billy in thanks, and turned to do the same with Freddie.

The phone kept ringing.

Jannah picked up the receiver, listened without speaking, then returned to the room. 'Cody it's for you.'

'Who is it; no one knows I'm here?'

'Well somebody does.' Jannah led Cody to her office. The somebody was Cody's CIA station chief. Cody closed the door and took the call. A few minutes later he found his champagne glass, emptied it in one gulp, filled it immediately and turned to the gathering.

'Can I have your attention please?' Cody waited for the noise level to drop and people to pause in their celebrations. He spoke. 'That phone call. We've had a job offer. Apparently there's a need for a group of talented, skilful, daring, devil may care, men and women to operate outside the law, a group to go on top secret missions; missions that will be fraught with danger but extremely well paid. Every single person in this room is recruited. What do you say?'

A wall of sound was the deafening response.

***

The bus had reached a quiet stretch of road near the fishponds by the Seletar turn off on the Upper Changi Road. The driver was thinking about going home to be with his family. The boys in the back were singing and playing jokes on one another, full of elation and good cheer. They relished their triumph with every fibre of their young, talented and beautiful lives.

The driver, who had travelled this road so often and could do it almost blind folded, left the image of his evening meal and glass of beer, to concentrate on the road ahead. There must have been an accident ahead because there was no traffic coming towards him. When he glanced into his rear view mirror, there was no traffic behind either.

The road had been closed in both directions. The bus was alone on the road.

The bomb had such power that it stopped the bus in its tracks tossing it high in the air like a child's toy. The explosion created a ball of searing flame. The scarred chassis chunked back to earth, sparks flying, windows blown out, rubber tyres alight, debris flying skyward and in all directions. Screams of agony filled the air.

Screams silenced by short bursts of machine gun fire.

***

'Sir, we're getting reports of an attack on the Changi road. A bus destroyed by a bomb. No survivors. Twenty three bodies accounted for. Twenty of the Singapore Defence Force, the driver and the two perpetrators, members of the Indonesian Marine Corps. They had their I.D. on them; Ade Budiman and Ridwan Suriya. The strange thing is that the two

Indonesians had been shot in the back.'

Freddie's boss replied in a monotone, without surprise, the words flowing from a single breath, emotionless.

'What a terrible thing to happen, how awful, at least we know who's to blame for this outrage. Well, you know the saying.

Dead men don't tell tales.'

ONE DEGREE NORTH
WEAVING FICTION FROM FACT
AUTHOR'S NOTE

In the beginning, after months of research and searching for inspiration, my fingers hit the keyboard and I started to write. I was incredibly fortunate. I had Penny, Maria, Steve and Tom reading the book as it was being written chapter by chapter, not knowing what the next would bring. Now that the story is complete, it seemed like a good idea to highlight some of the facts from which the fiction flowed. One Degree North is securely rooted in reality. Let's start at the very first scene: the ambush.

Women played a major front line role fighting for the Malayan Communist Party during the Malayan Emergency as well as being mothers, daughters, wives and lovers. They often took command and were inventive and effective fighters. Jannah's character was inspired by these women. The Ferret Force existed. The name came from their function to 'ferret out' the enemy and wreak havoc. This devastating British counter insurgency unit lasted only six months before being disbanded. Their tactics were thought to be too unconventional for the British High Command and for politicians' taste back in the United Kingdom. Dayaks, Borneo head-hunters were indeed used by the force as jungle trackers to find MCP camps for the Ferret Force to set ambushes of annihilation. Even though the Malayan Emergency was officially ended in July 1960, it took until 1989 for some guerrilla fighters to finally lay down their arms.

From December 1962 to August 1966 a small undeclared war (it was a war in military terms but not declared as one politically) between Indonesia and Malaysia became known as the Indonesian Confrontation or Konfrontasi took place. General Sukarno, President of Indonesia, wanted to annexe the northern territories of the island of Borneo - Sabah and Sarawak - from Malaysia and, if possible, to gain control of Brunei to unify the island under Indonesian Rule. The southern part of Borneo known as Kalimantan, was already part of Indonesia. The conflict drew in armed forces from Malaysia, Singapore, Britain, Australia and New Zealand. Insurgents who were responsible for the first raid into Brunei in the December of 1962 expanded their attacks to the eastern Malaya peninsula and the island of Singapore, up to and including 1965, the year of our story. The confrontation was a regional territorial dispute set against the growing communist influence in South East Asia and Singapore, lying at the crossroads to the Far East and a vital outpost against communism, had to be defended by the western powers.

The dramatic account of the BOAC 707 coming into land at Paya Lebah airport that opened Chapter 2 actually happened. During my research, I was given an account of that night by a passenger on the flight. She told of the arcing tracer fire snaking up to the plane during its descent, and of the cool presence of mind by the BOAC stewardess. Similarly, the bombing at the Katong Grange Hotel was real but was further dramatised for the story. In reality, the bomb squad arrived in time and managed to defuse the explosives.

Also true was The Rolling Stones playing two shows, one at 6.45pm and the second at 8.45pm on the 16th February 1965 at the Badminton Hall in Singapore. This was the band's last show of their first Far East tour. The show was described as the Big Beat Show and The Stones were called the 'Wild Men from Richmond'. They certainly drove the audience of girls wild who were criticised for their loud screaming and excited behaviour by the amazed Singaporeans at the time. So, in the middle of turmoil and conflict, life went along as normal as possible on the island. It also showed that the Swinging 60s had hit Singapore like a zestful wave of youthful energy.

The details of the bombing of the HSBC bank in the MacDonald Building, Orchard Road, were taken directly from the Singapore Straits Times newspaper report the day after the attack. It was the twenty ninth and the biggest bomb to explode in the civilian areas of Singapore, set by members of the Indonesian Marine Corps.

The idea of the criminal underworld fighting an invader is based on truth. On the 15th of February 1942 the Allied Forces in Singapore surrendered to the invading Japanese army. The Japanese harboured particular resentment against the Chinese people and many young men were executed in the first weeks of the occupation. During the Sook Ching Campaign (Purification through suffering) people accused of being anti-Japanese were systematically executed between 18th February and the 4th March 1942. The figure was estimated at 50,000 deaths in this three week period. Indeed Harry Lee, who later dropped the forename Harry to become known as Lee Kuan Yew the founding father of modern Singapore, was saved from death by his physical size. The Japanese wanted strong men for their work details. Harry Lee was singled out and survived. Those who did not make the grade were put in a lorry, taken to a nearby beach and shot. Resistance groups were formed within Singapore to mount guerrilla attacks to sabotage the Japanese. In the fictional One Degree North, the criminal underworld come together to fight the Indonesian invader.

The underworld was organised by territorial street gangs, each running gambling clubs, opium dens, brothels and protection rackets. It is believed that the era of these gangs has long past but in the 60s the gang culture was rife. Jonny Lau's 6-6-6 triad was a derivation of the powerful real life 3-6-9 gang. You can walk down Sago Lane today, the place of the death houses where Freddie met the street gang leaders at the meeting arranged by Jonny Lau. This was the actual place where coffins were carved, paper effigies of material belongings were made, and men and women nearing death waited for the afterlife on the cramped upper floors of the shophouses.

And so we arrive in Bugis Street. A street that served all sensory tastes. A street of earthly delights. Bugis Street was the haunt of the young and the beautiful of every sexual persuasion.

It was particularly known for the stunning women who were not women. Close to the harbour the street was crowded at night with crews from the merchantmen lying at anchor, curious businessmen and members of the Armed Forces who took the risk to flout the Out of Bounds notice. News of the arrival of the US naval ships on brief visits during a tour of duty in Vietnam caused frenetic excitement to every supplier of every kind of satisfaction, as they would be certain of a bumper payday as the thousands of crew members hit the streets of downtown Singapore.

Returning to the theme of fiction from fact, here's another real event that was woven into the storyline. In Chapter 7, Freddie and Cody along with Jannah take a daytrip on the yacht Galadriel. The whole episode minus our cast of fictional characters happened. Galadriel was owned by a real Freddie who was the template of our fictitious hero. Galadriel was first launched that day from the builder's yard and her shakedown cruise was from Singapore Harbour to Changi Yacht Club. The wind did drop. The engine did not start. Galadriel was swept out into the South China Sea. An RAF Shackleton located the drifting yacht and alerted the Singapore Defence Force who made the final rescue.

One Degree North draws to a close in May 1965, but the story doesn't end there. Throughout the summer of '65 the Indonesian Confrontation continues. On the evening of September 30th something momentous happened that changed history. Will Freddie and Company be called to action again?

ABOUT THE
AUTHOR

Years ago, Steve attended RAF Changi Grammar School in Singapore. It was here that he experienced living in a vibrantly exciting multi-cultural society and loved every minute. The memories of that time have stayed with him. The passage from a school boy living in an innocent childhood bubble to the awareness of adulthood has shaped the creation of One Degree North.

After college, Steve's first job was as an Account Executive at Young & Rubicam, an advertising agency. Steve continued in advertising for some years before taking a short break that lasted five years, during which he sailed the Atlantic Ocean from Gibraltar to Antigua and spent time in the music business as a roadie before becoming a rock group tour manager visiting Poland, Dubai and Zimbabwe to mention only a few gigs 'on the road'.

Steve's experience in business produced his first book 'Success before Start-Up'. The book was written to help people prepare for starting their own businesses. He drew on his own mistakes and successes in creating a new product in the gardening sector. Spanish Rings, Spanish style flower pot holders that create Mediterranean hanging gardens.

The company has grown into an international mail order concern.

In fiction, he has written a number of short stories. The titles are SCAM, CONTRA and HEADHUNTER. One Degree North is Steve's first novel. He has started work on One Degree South that continues the devilish ways of our heroes.